"Let me tell you, Jay Hammond. If you came in here with any intentions of having a roll in the sack for old times' sake, then you can think again."

He smiled. "And this from the woman who was begging me to marry her just eighteen months ago."

The mocking words made her temperature rise even farther. "I didn't beg you to marry me."

"Didn't you? Must have been some other raven-haired beauty."

"I suggested a business plan," she murmured tightly. Her cheeks felt as if they were on fire, her blood racing wildly through her body.

"So, are you making business plans with anyone else?" he murmured derisively. "Is that the question I should really be asking?"

BOOKS N THINGS
OF HARLINGEN
USED PAPERBACKS TRADED & SOLD
523 N. FIRST 425-5222
HARLINGEN, TX 78550
OPEN MON - SAT 10AM - 5PM

KATHRYN ROSS was born in Zambia, where her parents happened to live at the time. Educated in Ireland and England, she now lives in a village near Blackpool, England. Kathryn is a professional beauty therapist, but writing is her first love. As a child she wrote adventure stories, and at thirteen she was editor of her school magazine. Happily, ten writing years later *Designed with Love* was accepted by Harlequin. A romantic Sagittarian, she loves traveling to exotic locations.

**Look out for two books by
Kathryn Ross in October!**

**THE ITALIAN MARRIAGE is on sale in
Harlequin Presents**

**And the Presents Promotional program will
feature SCENT OF BETRAYAL in the
Sweet Revenge miniseries**

The Eleventh-Hour Groom

KATHRYN ROSS

THE MARRIAGE CONTRACT

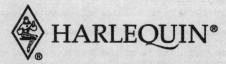

HARLEQUIN®

TORONTO • NEW YORK • LONDON
AMSTERDAM • PARIS • SYDNEY • HAMBURG
STOCKHOLM • ATHENS • TOKYO • MILAN • MADRID
PRAGUE • WARSAW • BUDAPEST • AUCKLAND

If you purchased this book without a cover you should be aware that this book is stolen property. It was reported as "unsold and destroyed" to the publisher, and neither the author nor the publisher has received any payment for this "stripped book."

ISBN 0-373-80536-5

THE ELEVENTH-HOUR GROOM

First North American Publication 2003.

Copyright © 2001 by Kathryn Ross.

All rights reserved. Except for use in any review, the reproduction or utilization of this work in whole or in part in any form by any electronic, mechanical or other means, now known or hereafter invented, including xerography, photocopying and recording, or in any information storage or retrieval system, is forbidden without the written permission of the publisher, Harlequin Enterprises Limited, 225 Duncan Mill Road, Don Mills, Ontario, Canada M3B 3K9.

All characters in this book have no existence outside the imagination of the author and have no relation whatsoever to anyone bearing the same name or names. They are not even distantly inspired by any individual known or unknown to the author, and all incidents are pure invention.

This edition published by arrangement with Harlequin Books S.A.

® and TM are trademarks of the publisher. Trademarks indicated with ® are registered in the United States Patent and Trademark Office, the Canadian Trade Marks Office and in other countries.

Visit us at www.eHarlequin.com

Printed in U.S.A.

CHAPTER ONE

ELIZABETH had been the one to propose marriage. So, if she had to apportion blame for the ensuing mayhem, she supposed, in fairness, that she had to shoulder some of the responsibility herself. But only a little...it was mostly his fault, of course. His fault for not loving her, for agreeing to something for all the wrong reasons.

When colleagues asked her how long her marriage had lasted and she answered six months, they always looked at her and shook their heads. 'Fancied a big white wedding, did you?'

'No, I just fancied him,' she would answer wryly. 'Big mistake.'

All those thoughts rushed through her head every time she opened her office drawer and saw the official looking manila envelope staring up at her from within. She imagined it was glaring at her reproachfully, which was rubbish, of course, how could an envelope be reproachful? Even so, she felt better after she had slammed the drawer shut on it again.

It had arrived by courier almost ten days ago and she had signed for it, thinking it was something to do with work. Only when she had really looked at it had she noticed the Jamaican postmark. Then she had recognised the handwriting.

It was from him and she was scared to open it. Scared because deep down she knew that envelope contained divorce papers.

Elizabeth Hammond, successful career girl, afraid of nothing and nobody...well, with the possible exception of heights and going to the doctor…was now afraid to open an envelope, she mocked herself. She needed to get a grip. She'd take it home tonight, pour herself a glass of wine and open it. Face her demons.

'Elizabeth, fancy a drink after work?' Robert asked as he passed her desk.

'Can't, Rob, sorry.' She hardly looked up at him. 'I've got a stack of paperwork to catch up on.'

'Tomorrow then,' he said easily.

The phone rang on her desk and she snatched it up, whilst at the same time glancing at her watch. She had an important meeting in ten minutes. 'Richmond Advertising Agency, Elizabeth Hammond speaking.' She sang the words breathily. 'How can I help?'

'You can help by signing the damn papers I sent you.' The familiar American tones of her estranged husband drawled wryly.

The busy office suddenly seemed to fade into oblivion. The noise of printers and telephones, people's voices and the London traffic outside all disappeared as if someone had pushed a mute button. Leaving only her, and Jay's voice at the end of a line.

'Elizabeth, don't you dare hang up on me,' he warned coolly as she made no reply.

The thought hadn't occurred to her until he said it, and then she was sorely tempted.

She took a deep breath. 'I'm busy, Jay,' she said briskly. She was pleased at how composed she sounded, as if it wasn't nearly twelve months since they had last spoken, as if his voice meant nothing.

'Yes, so am I,' he grated. 'Why haven't you signed the papers?'

'I haven't read them properly yet.' It wasn't entirely a lie, but she imagined she felt heat emanating from the drawer where they lay, untouched, unread.

'Are you being deliberately awkward?'

'No!'

'You could have fooled me,' he grated impatiently.

'No one could fool you, Jay.' She couldn't resist the dig. 'You're infallible, remember?'

There was a silence for a moment and she wished perversely that she hadn't said that. What was the point in quarrelling? She couldn't win with Jay, anyway…never had. And maybe he was right, maybe she was being deliberately awkward. She'd known from the moment she'd looked at the envelope that it contained divorce papers, and she had consciously put off opening it. It was wrong of her, she should sign them and get Jay Hammond out of her life, once and for all. After all, they'd been separated for a year, wasn't it time to move on?

'Listen, Jay, I—'

He cut across her conciliatory tones. 'What time do you finish work?'

'What?' She frowned. What had that to do with anything? Jay was in Jamaica; she was in London. Was he going to fax her something, she wondered in perplexity. 'Well…five-thirty—'

'I'll pick you up from outside the office. Don't be late.'

'Jay, I—' The dull monotone of a dead line droned in her ear now. He'd put the phone down. Panic zinged through her. It was as if someone had injected an overdose of adrenalin straight into a main artery. Jay was here in London! She felt sick with apprehension. She couldn't see him. It was more than she could deal with. Maybe she could tell everyone she was sick and go home and hide. Lock the door, take the phone off the hook, run away.

'You okay, Elizabeth?' A voice seemed to be coming from a long way away. 'Elizabeth…wakey, wakey.' It droned on sarcastically. 'You've got a meeting with the boss in five minutes. Aren't you up to it?'

She looked up at Colin Watson. He was about thirty-five, tall and not bad-looking if it hadn't been for the smug expression on his face. Elizabeth really didn't like him. The guy had been gunning for her job for three months now and he was trying his best to undermine her at every turn. He'd just love her to go home and let him take over the meeting. She could just imagine him talking to their boss. *Elizabeth's got women's troubles,* he would say with a patronising sneer. *I'll take over, John. Leave it all to me. Then we can just discuss it over a game of golf next week.* Yes, she knew how Colin Watson operated.

Elizabeth looked at him now and wanted to swear. But Elizabeth Hammond never swore. She went home and took a few herbal relaxing tablets and sweated herself into a lather of work—work that, thankfully, was always a hundred times better than his.

She forced a smile to her lips now. She'd have to be dying before she let chauvinistic Colin get one over on her. 'I'm just on my way, Colin,' she said brightly, collecting her work. 'It's all in hand.'

The meeting should have lasted an hour, but dragged on for three. Elizabeth's ideas on the new soap powder advertising campaign were thrashed out as if they were talking about a cure for cancer, though she managed to refrain from looking at her watch until it was all finished. If John had seen her even glancing at the time he'd have thought she was less than one hundred per cent committed. And that was the biggest crime anyone could perpetrate as far as her boss was concerned.

Only when she had packed everything away did she dare look at the time. Nearly five o'clock. If she hurried, she could leave early and avoid Jay. She couldn't see him today. Her head was pounding and she was exhausted. Besides, she should really open that envelope and study the contents before talking to her husband. She'd have to acquaint herself with the terms of their divorce before she could agree to anything.

She zipped up her laptop in its travel case and tucked a few papers and her mobile phone in with it. 'I'm going to go home, John.' She tossed the words casually over at him. 'I want to study these details in the peace and quiet of my own office.'

He nodded. 'Fine. See you eight-thirty tomorrow. Perhaps you'll have the draft on the Menda account finished by then?'

Elizabeth recognised the words as a command, not a request. She knew her boss well enough to know he would expect that work on his desk first thing.

'No problem.' She smiled at Colin as she swept past him. Despite his numerous attempts to hijack her presentation, it had gone well. She knew that just by looking at the disgruntled expression on his face.

She picked up the manila envelope from her drawer and pushed it into her case with the rest of her work. Tonight, not only had she to read divorce papers, she had to prepare another account. And all she really felt like doing was going to bed and drawing the covers over her head.

Don't be pathetic, Elizabeth, she told herself angrily. Your marriage was over before it started. Paperwork isn't going to change anything.

Before leaving the building she visited the cloakroom. Re-applied perfume and lipstick, then studied the pallor of her reflection whilst running a comb through her short dark hair.

So what if her personal life was a disaster area? she told herself briskly. At least she had a successful career.

So why did she feel so heavy-hearted? Why did the envelope in her briefcase seem, metaphorically speaking, to weigh a ton? Maybe it was because it was her thirtieth birthday tomorrow, and thirty did sound so much older than twenty-nine. She was getting old and getting a divorce all at the same time. It was a bit depressing.

She put on her long grey overcoat and lifted up her briefcase. Endings were always painful, she told herself. That was all it was. She didn't love Jay any more. She'd face the end and then start afresh with someone else, someone who loved her. And she'd look on her thirtieth birthday as a new beginning.

She ran to catch one of the lifts waiting in the corridor, just managing to get in before the doors swished shut. She glanced again at her watch as it descended the six floors to ground level. She was twenty minutes early. She'd avoid Jay, catch the tube and then lock the front door of her apartment. And if he did come round she wouldn't answer the bell, no matter how many times he pressed it. She'd see him when *she* was ready, not before.

The doors opened smoothly into the marble and glass foyer. And there he was, standing like a sentinel by the front exit into Oxford Street.

First of all she felt shocked. Then she felt numb as their eyes met. Anger and pain were suspended in a brief moment when she found herself acknowledging how handsome he was. So attractive that she felt her heart go into overdrive, just like it used to do in the days when she'd had a major crush on him.

He had dark hair and was tall, well over six feet, with a broad athletic build, that was somehow accentuated by the dark overcoat he wore over his suit. His tanned skin was in stark contrast to the grey February day. The dark eyes that seemed to pierce into hers made her blanch.

She wondered if she could pretend she hadn't seen him and step smartly away from him through the side door. Once into Oxford Street she could merge with the crowds. He'd never catch her.

'Ms Hammond, you have a visitor,' the receptionist

called out, bringing her back to reality. 'I was just about to phone up to your office.'

'Okay, thanks.' Elizabeth smiled wanly at the woman and walked across towards her husband on legs that felt decidedly wobbly.

His gaze seemed to take in everything about her in those few moments. Her smart grey business suit, the silk stockings, the height of her heels, before sweeping back to catch and hold her blue eyes.

'Hello, Beth,' he said smoothly.

'Hi.'

There was silence then, silence when all she could hear was her heart beating in her ears. She wished he wouldn't look at her like that. As if he could see straight into her soul and know the truth.

You're nearly thirty, she told herself, trying to get a grip on her emotions. This man should no longer be able to make you feel like a tongue-tied adolescent. You don't love him any more.

Some other members of staff came out of the lifts behind them.

'Bye, Elizabeth,' they chorused as they passed her. 'See you in the morning.'

'Yes…bye.' She glanced over at them, the distraction helping to ease some of the tension inside her. They were secretaries from her office, but they weren't looking at Elizabeth, they were looking at Jay, open admiration shining from their eyes.

Some things never changed, she thought wryly.

'Right, well shall we go?' Jay asked suddenly.

She looked back at him. 'Go where?'

'I thought we'd have dinner together, talk in a civilised manner.'

Talk over dinner? Elizabeth wanted to laugh. She felt so self-conscious around him that it was an effort to even breathe, never mind pretend to force food down her throat. 'What are you doing here, Jay?'

'You know why I'm here.'

He took hold of her arm and with a polite smile over at the receptionist who was watching them with avid curiosity, steered Elizabeth out through the revolving doors.

The cold blast of the winter day was biting after the central heating in the office. She pulled her coat further around her slender body, and made to turn away from Jay. He wouldn't release her arm. His grip was so tight that it hurt.

'Will you let go of me?' she whispered furiously, her eyes blazing as she looked up at him.

'We're going for dinner.' He steered her towards a car waiting by the kerb on double yellow lines.

'I'm not going anywhere with you.'

'Yes, you are.' He opened the door and stood waiting for her to get into the passenger seat.

'You've got a damn nerve, Jay Hammond, turning up here out of the blue and expecting me to just fall in with your wishes. Let me tell you that I've got more important things to be doing.'

'Yes, I'm sure you have. But I've flown halfway around the world to talk to you.'

'Well that's your problem. And will you let go of my arm? You're hurting me.'

'Sorry.' He released her immediately and she rubbed her arm, glaring at him reproachfully.

'Look, I realise that you are a busy woman. I know it's probably a shock my turning up like this. But I need to talk to you, Beth…it's urgent.'

She hesitated.

'So, what do you say?' he murmured. 'Will you give me a few hours of your time…please?'

Hell, he wasn't going to start being nice to her, was he?

She could handle his disdain, his arrogance, but she couldn't hack it if he started to be kind. That led to all sorts of dangerous grey areas.

Her eyes moved over the handsome face. It was hard to tell what he was thinking, his features were impassive.

She sighed. 'Okay, but I've only got an hour. I've got work to do.'

'Thanks.' He smiled. 'I appreciate it.'

He held the door for her as she got in. She told herself she was only doing this to avoid a scene. Her work colleagues would be coming out at any moment and she didn't want them asking her questions tomorrow.

He slammed the door and then came around to join her.

She watched as he fastened his safety belt then checked his mirror before pulling out into the steady stream of traffic.

This was really weird, she thought. If anyone had told her this morning that Jay would pick her up from work she would have looked at them as if they were mad.

'So…you haven't really come all this way just to see me…have you?' she asked cautiously.

He glanced over at her. 'Yes. I have.'

She wanted to ask why, but she couldn't. She was too afraid he was going to say the dreaded D word. But of course that had to be the reason. What other one was there? He wanted a divorce.

She noticed the familiar tang of his aftershave. It made a curl of remembrance stir painfully inside her. She squashed it immediately.

'Where did you get the car?' she asked, more for something to say than anything else.

'I rented it.'

'Where are you staying?'

'I don't know. I haven't booked in anywhere yet.'

She frowned. 'You mean you've just arrived?'

He nodded. 'Yep. I rang you from the airport.'

'Oh!' She wished she could think straight.

She watched as he drove into an underground car park. Watched the reflection of the neon lights as they played over the hard contours of his face.

He parked and then turned to look at her. 'I've booked a table at a restaurant around the corner.'

'You've booked a restaurant but you haven't booked a hotel?'

He shrugged and grinned. 'I can think better on a full stomach.'

She stared at him, trying to work this out. But her brain was befuddled with confusing, sidetracking thoughts, like how his smile lit up his eyes, how his lips were firm and yet sensual, how the shape of his face was hard-boned and square, giving him a look of arrogant determination.

Sometimes in her dreams she had imagined seeing him again, had imagined what it might be like. Sometimes she had thought that she would feel nothing and sometimes her body had twisted with an empty kind of longing. Now she didn't know what her body was telling her, except how wonderful he looked…and that was crazy.

'Elizabeth.' His eyes seemed to be resting on her lips. 'Are you okay?'

'Of course I'm okay.' She wrenched her gaze away from him. Picked up her briefcase and opened the car door. 'I'm hungry,' she lied. 'Like you, I can't think on an empty stomach.'

CHAPTER TWO

THE restaurant which was one of the best in town was a place that Elizabeth had only ever visited when she had been entertaining clients for the firm. And even then she hadn't got one of the tables in the private side booths; they were always reserved weeks in advance.

'How did you get this table?' Elizabeth asked as the waiter disappeared with their coats and they settled themselves opposite each other in the private alcove.

'I just bribed the head waiter,' he answered nonchalantly.

Her eyes widened. 'Really? I didn't see you.'

He grinned as he handed her a menu, and she realised he was teasing her.

For a moment their eyes held. Then she felt his gaze sweeping over her, assessing the heart-shaped face, the sophisticated style of her raven-dark hair, the slender lines of her figure.

'You're looking well,' he murmured.

'Thanks.' She gave him a strained smile. 'So are you.' They sounded like two strangers, she thought. Who would believe that they had once promised to love, honour and stay together, forsaking all others? Her lips twisted wryly as she reminded herself what a sham that had been.

'You've cut your hair,' he remarked.

She put a hand self-consciously to the short, urchin cut, remembering that he had once told her how much he liked her waist long hair. 'It got a bit hard to manage.'

A glimmer of a smile lit his dark eyes. 'Pity…I always liked your hair.'

Meaning he didn't like it now? Well, she didn't care, she told herself crossly. In fact part of the reason she'd had cut it was because she knew he had liked it. She had finished worrying about what Jay did and didn't like. That game was over long ago.

'It's been a long time…hasn't it,' he remarked casually. 'Must be what…nearly a year?'

It was over a year, but she wasn't about to admit she was counting. 'Something like that. How are things in Jamaica?'

'Hot.' He smiled. 'Do you miss it?'

Of course she missed it. Although she was originally from England her parents had moved to the Caribbean when she was just nine. In her heart Jamaica was still home. But she wouldn't admit to Jay that she felt homesick. She had moved away because of him, because of their sham of a marriage. She had to put a brave face on things. So she just smiled and shrugged. 'Sometimes,' she said easily.

The wine waiter interrupted them to ask what they'd like to drink.

'Would you like wine, or something stronger?' Jay asked her.

'A glass of white wine would be fine, thank you.'

Jay ordered a bottle, then settled back in his chair again.

She shouldn't really drink, she told herself. She needed to keep a clear head.

He looked remarkably fresh and healthy considering he had just made a ten-hour transatlantic flight, she thought.

He leaned back in the chair, stretching his long legs, looking the epitome of well-honed manhood, muscular, yet trim, broad and strong, arrogantly relaxed. She was pleased to note a few grey strands amid the dark thickness of his hairs.

He was getting older, she told herself. Good…maybe

one day women would stop finding him so attractive. If there were any justice in the world, maybe one day he would know what unrequited love felt like. And serve him right, she told herself darkly. He might even look back on his life and say, If only I hadn't let Beth go. She was the only woman who truly loved me. And meanwhile she would be living with a hunky guy who worshipped the ground she walked on. And she would laugh and say. I'm glad I left Jay.

He leaned forward, and Beth snapped out of the ludicrous daydream, feeling foolish. Jay was only thirty-seven, and losing his looks was probably something he would never have to worry about. There was no justice in the world. What was more, he was the one who wanted a divorce, which must mean there was someone else in his life...someone serious.

Was he planning to marry Lisa? The question twisted painfully inside.

'So, I take it life in London is as wonderful as you thought it would be?'

'Better than wonderful,' she found herself gushing. 'I absolutely adore it.'

'Really?' His voice held a hint of dry irony. 'Well, I'm glad you haven't been disappointed.'

Beth's eyes narrowed. 'This is all very cosy, Jay, but, at the risk of sounding rude, I'm sure you haven't come all this way to make idle chit-chat with me. Do you want to cut to the bottom line?'

'You know the bottom line. I want you to sign those papers,' he said calmly. 'Why haven't you?'

She avoided his eyes. 'I just haven't got around to it, that's all.'

The waiter brought their wine and poured it for Jay to taste, before filling up their glasses.

A piano struck up at the other side of the room, a relaxing romantic melody that blended with the gentle hum of conversation around them, but was at discomforting odds with their situation.

'Are you ready to order?' Jay asked as another waiter approached.

'Yes.' She ordered with the briefest glance at the menu, choosing a salad, her usual preference when she came here on business.

Then she snapped the menu closed and handed it back with a smile. She would pretend this was a business deal. She could handle those. 'I'm surprised you remember London well enough to select this restaurant. How long ago is it since you were here?'

'About seven months.'

She'd expected him to say seven years, because she knew he had visited London before they first met. It was a shock, therefore, to know he'd been here and hadn't looked her up.

'Oh?' She took a sip of her wine. Well, why should he look her up? she told herself. He'd only do that if, like now, he wanted something. It wasn't as if he missed her, or that they were even still friends.

'I was here on business. I'm designing a craft for the round the world yacht race.'

'The boat yard is doing well, then?' she asked idly.

He frowned. 'Beth, you are still a sleeping partner in the business. I send you cheques every quarter, direct to your bank account. You know how the business is doing.'

She shrugged. In truth she never looked at that money; she didn't want it. It felt like blood money.

'You don't have to pretend. I know how much that money means to you,' he grated quietly. 'And I suppose the reason you won't sign my papers is monetary as well.'

'I'm sorry to disappoint you, Jay, but I don't need your money. I'm an independent, successful career woman.'

'Well, you like to play at being one, anyway,' he said suddenly, impatiently.

'I'm not playing, Jay. I am independent.'

'May I remind Elizabeth Hammond that she wouldn't be where she is today if it wasn't for my help,' he grated mockingly.

'And you wouldn't be where you are today if it wasn't for my help,' she retorted, her eyes flashing fire. 'Our arrangement was to our mutual benefit, and don't you forget it.'

'Well, that took all of, what, fifteen minutes?' He glanced at his watch. 'And we are right back to the same argument we were having a year ago.'

'You started it,' Beth murmured.

'No. You started it when you proposed marriage to me,' he reminded her grimly.

'I didn't propose marriage; I proposed a business merger.' With difficulty she kept the colour from flooding into her face. 'And I wouldn't have done it except for the fact that I was desperate and I thought you were my friend. I also thought you were a gentleman. It seems I was wrong on both counts.'

'Maybe I'm not much of a gentleman.' He shrugged and sat back in his chair. 'But I was your friend.'

She noted his use of the past tense and felt her heart heavy against her chest. She had ruined everything. Once upon a time Jay had liked her. They had been friends. Now he looked on her with contempt. He thought she was money-orientated; he thought she had used him. She supposed she was guilty of being greedy, but her greed had nothing much to do with money. Her greed had been to want more than Jay's friendship. She had wanted him to love her, as she had loved him. But because of her pride she had gone about it the wrong way. Used the terms of her father's will to provide a convenient excuse.

She remembered clearly the day she had made the outrageous proposal. They had been sitting at the beach bar. She had ordered a rum punch, downed it quickly and ordered a second.

'It's not like you to drink in the middle of the afternoon,' he had remarked softly. 'I know you are upset about your dad's death, but this isn't the answer.'

'So what's the answer then?' she asked.

'I don't know. Henry's death is a shock; you must still be reeling from it. Coming to terms with his will on top of that must be hard.' Jay shook his head. 'I can't believe that he actually went ahead and made out his will the way he did.'

'Can't you?' Elizabeth's tone was dry. 'You know what a strong character he was. How stubborn he could be when he got an idea in his head. He always made it clear that his dearest wish was for you and I to get together.'

'Yes, I suppose he did,' Jay said thoughtfully. 'In the two years I worked for him, I don't think a day went by without him mentioning your name in a very positive way to me.' For a moment a gleam of humour lit Jay's dark eyes. 'We used to find his matchmaking antics amusing, didn't we, Beth? But this is going some even by his tenacious standards.'

'Let's not go through all that.' Beth cut across him hastily, cringing with embarrassment. Jay might have found her father's matchmaking attempts amusing but they had always flustered her. They'd been too near the mark, too near what she wished for secretly in her heart. Whether her father had realised her feelings or just thought their union would make sound economical sense, she had no idea; she just hoped that Jay didn't perceive how she felt. That would be too humiliating by far.

Elizabeth tried to sound cool and objective. 'The fact is that he did make his will out with the clear purpose of pushing us together, and if I don't marry you within seven weeks the boat yard, plus a substantial sum of money, go to my stepmother, along with everything else.'

'Cheryl will probably see that you are well provided for. I'm sure your father will have left her very well off. The boat yard is just a tiny proportion of your father's assets.'

'Cheryl will be all right. But that's not the point is it?' Beth retorted, hurt beyond words. 'I shouldn't have to ask for what is rightfully mine.'

'Well, there's not much you can do about that, is there?'

'Aren't you worried about your job?' Beth tried a new track. If he wasn't worried about her, maybe he was worried about his own position.

'Not really. I suppose Cheryl will keep me on.'

'If she has any sense.' Beth tried to implant some doubt in his mind. Though she knew full well that her stepmother was well aware that without Jay the boat yard would go downhill fast. Not only was he a talented designer, he ran the place with extreme efficiency. Her father had tried to get him to buy into the business on many occasions, just to keep him there, but Jay had always refused the offers.

'Anyway I've been offered another job,' he said suddenly.

'What?' Beth sat straighter in her chair. 'Where? Here, on the island?'

Jay grinned. 'No. The Bahamas.'

Those words shocked her more than her father's will. The thought that Jay would leave was unbearable.

'They've made me a good offer. I think I'm going to accept it, subject to a few loose ends here—'

'You can't!' She stared at him in horror.

'Why not?'

'Because I think you should stay here and marry me.'

She remembered the silence that had followed her

words. The way Jay had looked at her, the quizzical lift of his eyebrow.

'Call me old-fashioned, Beth,' he drawled, 'but, where I come from in the States, it's usual for the men to propose to the women—'

'Don't be facetious, Jay. I'm proposing a business deal,' she stipulated quickly. She remembered sounding confident, she remembered holding the darkness of his eyes with a direct gaze. 'If you marry me, I'll sign half the business over to you and we can share the profits.'

'I never realised you were so business-orientated,' Jay drawled, sitting back in his chair and staring at her as if he had never seen her before.

She shrugged. 'Maybe you don't really know me that well.'

'Maybe I don't.'

'So what do you say?'

'I don't know. I'll have to think about it.'

He hadn't even wanted her wrapped up with gifts...that had stung. Only for the rum kicking in, blocking out the pain, she might have grinned and let it go, said she'd been joking. 'Okay, I'll give you a sixty-forty split, seeing as you will be doing most of the work,' she found herself saying instead. 'That's my last offer.'

'So, let's just get this straight. You are suggesting that we get married to fulfil the terms of your father's will. Then what?' His eyes narrowed. 'A quickie divorce a few weeks later when the business has been signed over?'

'No!' She frowned. 'We can't do that. Dad stipulated in his will that we should live together and stay married for at least a year.'

'Good old Henry thought of everything, didn't he?' Jay murmured sardonically. 'Did he stipulate instructions for our sleeping arrangements as well?'

The heat of embarrassment seared through her. Before

she could think of a suitably sarcastic reply he went swiftly on. 'So how long do you want to play this charade for?'

'I don't know.' She shrugged. 'Do we have to put a date on it? After all, it's not as if either of us are serious about anyone else, is it? Shall we just see how things go?'

There was a moment's silence, a moment when he just stared at her and she felt incredibly foolish...

'Okay.' His agreement when it came nearly bowled her off the seat in surprise. 'But if we get married we do it properly.'

'How do you mean?'

'We sign a premarital contract.' Suddenly he was the one dictating conditions. 'We put the terms of our marriage down in black and white.'

'Fine,' she agreed airily.

'And I'll buy into the business.'

'There's no need—you'll automatically own half of it once we're married—'

Jay cut across her. 'I don't want something for nothing, Elizabeth. Anyway, we can use the money to invest in the boat yard. It needs updating.'

It had only been when she had sobered up that she had wondered about the sanity of the situation.

And now, nearly eighteen months down the line, older and wiser she sat opposite him across this dinner table and wished that she had never gone through with the charade. But it was too late for regrets.

The waiter brought their food. Elizabeth toyed with the meal for a while. She had absolutely no appetite.

'Did I tell you that Cheryl is getting married again?' Jay said suddenly. 'She wrote to tell me about it last week. Or rather to tell us about it... She still thinks we are together.'

Beth's eyes widened. 'Who is she marrying?'

Jay shrugged. 'I don't know. I think she said his name was Alan. She met him on a cruise.'

Elizabeth smiled. 'Well, I'm glad she's found happiness again. I know she missed Dad terribly.' In fact Cheryl had felt so lonely in the house she had once shared with Elizabeth's father that she had sold up soon after his death and moved back to the States. She was living in Florida now.

'She's invited us to the wedding.' Jay told her.

'Really? In Florida?'

Jay shook his head. 'She's coming back to Jamaica to get married. They're having a wedding and honeymoon package. Getting married on the beach.'

'Like we did.' The words slipped out.

'Yes.' His eyes moved over her face thoughtfully. 'You were the eleven o'clock bride,' he said. 'Do you remember? They'd posted the notice on the hotel board, between the times of the diving lessons.'

She smiled. That red-hot day in Jamaica was etched on her memory for all time. The gentle sea breeze billowing her veil behind her. The scent of the tropical flowers, the calm turquoise waters of the Caribbean lapping against the sugar-white sand. 'Of course I remember. We both laughed about it...said we were the ones taking the deepest plunge of all.'

'Wasn't that deep a plunge, though, was it?' he remarked wryly. 'Six months. People get longer than that for robbery.'

'We may have only been together for six months, but we're still married,' she reminded him, then wondered why she'd felt the need to say that.

'What's the matter: frightened that your stepmother might contest the will because we didn't stay together for the stipulated twelve months?' he drawled wryly.

'Don't be ridiculous; Cheryl wouldn't do something like that. She was never interested in the boat yard, anyway.'

'Which was why you felt you could safely leave after

six months I suppose.' There was a hard, mocking edge to Jay's tone. 'You had it all figured out, didn't you, Beth?'

He made her sound so calculating, but nothing could have been further from the truth. She had taken a gamble when she had married him, a gamble that one day he might feel something for her, fall for her the way she had for him. It had been a wild, impossibly romantic dream destined to just bring her pain. She shook her head. 'No, Jay. That was the problem,' she told him quietly. 'I didn't have anything figured out. I just made a mistake. Marriage is too important to reduce it to a mere business venture.'

His features were impassive, his eyes dark, remote. 'You've got some cool nerve to lecture on the principles of marriage, Beth. May I remind you that the "business venture" was your idea. You proposed it, talked me into it, then walked out on it.'

'Because it was a mistake.' She held his gaze for as long as she could, then had to look away.

What was he thinking? she wondered. Probably about the fact that, financially, she had done all right out of the situation.

She shrugged. Maybe it was best to leave his opinion of her where it was. Better that than him knowing how much she had loved him, she thought suddenly. He'd find that really amusing.

She reached for her wine and took a hasty sip. 'Anyway I'll have to write to Cheryl, tell her we've split up,' she continued briskly. 'I've been meaning to write for quite some time, but I keep putting it off.'

'I've brought her letter with me.' Jay reached into his inside jacket pocket and brought out the letter, passing it across the table to her. 'I thought you'd want to read it. Her new address and telephone number are on there as well.'

'Thanks.' She put it away in her handbag. Then went back to toying with her food.

She felt somehow mollified when she noticed that Jay hadn't eaten much of his meal either. He must be tired, she thought suddenly. The jet lag travelling from the Caribbean to Europe was quite bad.

'How long are you planning on staying?' she asked him abruptly.

'Long enough for you to sign the papers.' He looked over at her pointedly. 'I want to bring them back with me.'

She nodded and straightened her cutlery on the plate, giving up on the pretence of eating. 'I'll sign them tonight.'

'Thanks.'

So that was it, then, she thought, it was the end of the marriage. And it had been reasonably civil: no shouting, no recriminations...well, not many. Just a stack of paperwork to sign. Somewhere inside she felt like crying.

'Would you like pudding, or a coffee?' Jay asked as their plates were taken away.

'No thanks.' She glanced at her watch. 'I should be going. I really have got work to do.'

'I'll drive you home.' Jay raised his hand to gain the waiter's attention.

They didn't speak again until they were back in the car, driving along the darkened streets. Things were quieter now, the rush hour over, the hectic scrabble to get out of the city finished.

She directed him to her home, trying not to let her mind skip ahead to the future. Once the divorce papers were signed, would she ever see him again?

He stopped the car outside the mews where she had an apartment and looked over at her.

Silence hung heavily between them. He noticed how the streetlight played over her features. She looked incredibly pale. The Elizabeth he had known had always had a golden tan. It had been a surprise to see how fair her complexion was, quite a beautiful contrast against the raven darkness of her hair.

His gaze lingered for a moment on the softness of her lips. She moistened them.

Did he make her nervous? he wondered suddenly. Did he still have the power to turn her on?

'You've got something in your hair,' he murmured, reaching out to brush a finger through a wisp of her silky hair at an imaginary speck.

He watched how she reacted to his touch, noting the faint blush that appeared high on her cheekbones, the almost imperceptible shiver as his fingers made contact with her skin.

He pulled back, a curl of satisfaction stirring inside him. The idea that he still had some power over her senses pleased him. Why was that? he wondered. Was it because he was still angry with her for walking out so soon after their marriage? She had certainly dented his pride when she had left, and there was a small part of him that would like to settle that score.

'Are you going to invite me in?' he asked softly.

He noticed how she swallowed nervously.

'That way, I can wait while you sign my papers.'

He watched her very carefully; there was a flicker of annoyance in the bright blue of her eyes before she swiftly turned her head away. He smiled. If he played things carefully, maybe he could have a little sporting pleasure before ending things. Do a little damage to her pride.

She pulled her coat further around her body. His impatience to finish things grated on raw nerves. She wondered if his sudden haste to get a divorce meant he was planning on marrying again straight away.

She thought about asking him, but then couldn't bring herself to form the question.

A few snowflakes twirled down onto the windscreen from the darkened sky. Maybe he was just in a hurry to get back to Jamaica, she thought. And really she couldn't blame him.

'Come on in,' she said resignedly. 'I'll make us a coffee.' She reached for her briefcase.

'Oh, hell!' She scrabbled frantically in the dark space at her feet.

'What is it?'

'My briefcase isn't here!' She scrabbled even more frantically, her fingers locking on nothing more than her handbag.

'Don't panic, it has to be somewhere.' Jay switched on the overhead light. 'Did you bring it into the restaurant with you?'

She closed her eyes, willing herself to remember. 'Yes…yes, I did.' She remembered putting it under the table. Then she remembered picking it up as they made to leave. She frowned. 'I think I put it down when the waiter helped me on with my coat. I must have left it in the restaurant! How stupid of me.'

She couldn't believe she had done such a thing. She was usually so methodical, so level-headed. But her mind had been on Jay, on the divorce. Her eyes widened. 'The papers you want me to sign are in there.' She remembered suddenly.

His eyes narrowed. 'Are you doing this on purpose?' The soothing note had gone from his voice now, she noted.

'No, of course not. My laptop computer is in there as well.' She groaned. 'And my mobile phone. What a nightmare!' She reached for the door handle. 'I better ring the restaurant, see if they still have it.'

Jay locked the car and followed her through the green Georgian door into her ground-floor apartment.

She was glad she had tidied up this morning before going to work. The pretty apartment with its terracotta carpets and cream furnishings looked immaculate as she flicked on the side lamps.

She took out the phone book and flicked hurriedly through it, aware as she did so of Jay wandering around the lounge, picking up some framed photos on the mantelpiece. Some were old ones, taken when her mum was alive. Some from more recent years were of her father and Cheryl's wedding day.

Her phone call was answered and she turned her attention to the foreign accent at the other end.

Jay wandered over to the other side of the room, noting the fact that there was a kitchen, a bathroom and just one double bedroom. His eyes lingered for a moment on her bed, lit by a single shaft of light from the open doorway.

For a moment he found himself remembering her words in the restaurant, Marriage is too important to reduce it to a mere business venture. She hadn't thought like that when she had given herself to him in the marital bed, he reflected angrily.

He turned around and watched her as she spoke on the phone. He noted her long, slender fingers were devoid of the plain wedding band she had once worn.

She smiled at him and covered the receiver with her hand. 'They have my briefcase, Jay,' she said happily.

'Well, what a relief!' he drawled sardonically.

'Yes…isn't it?' She glanced away from him uncertainly, and continued with her conversation.

'They close at twelve,' she said a few minutes later as she put the receiver down. 'And I said I'd collect it tonight.'

Jay glanced at his watch. 'I'll collect it for you.'

'Would you?' She met his eyes gratefully, wondering if she had imagined the derisive tone in his voice a few moments ago. 'It's just that if I set out to do it I'll have to take two tubes across the city.'

'It's no problem.' He nodded. 'There will just be the small fee of a coffee and the use of your phone so I can book a hotel room.'

'You've got yourself a deal.' She took off her coat and walked through to the small, modern kitchen. 'Help yourself to the phone book,' she called to him.

When she brought the tray of coffee back through to the lounge Jay was just putting the phone down.

'Did you find a hotel?'

'Yes, I got the one I stayed in last time.'

She wondered if he had been on his own the last time he'd come to London on business. Maybe he had brought Lisa? She was his secretary…amongst other things. He could have combined business with pleasure…he was good at that.

She veered her mind away from that particular direction. 'It's snowing pretty heavily outside now,' she remarked lightly as she put the tray down.

'Yes.' He stood with his back to her looking out of the window. 'Let's hope we don't get snowed in.'

'I don't think there is much chance of that.' She went to stand beside him. 'It doesn't usually stick.'

He looked down at her. 'Pity,' he drawled, a teasing light in his eye. 'We could have warmed ourselves by the fire and reminisced over the good old days.'

'What good old days?' She tried to make her voice flippant.

'Oh, come on, Beth.' He shook his head and turned to face her. 'We did have some good times together,' he said gently. 'Surely you haven't forgotten?'

She felt her heart miss a beat, felt suddenly breathless

as she met the velvet darkness of his eyes. Then she looked hurriedly away, confusion clouding any memories.

He reached out a hand, tipping her chin, forcing her to look up at him.

The touch of his hand on her skin made her tremble. Very slowly he allowed his hand to move caressingly down the side of her neck.

The sensation made a shiver of awareness tingle through her body. She felt rooted to the spot, unable to think, unable to even breathe properly.

She felt his gaze resting on her mouth. It was almost like a physical caress, she could feel her lips tingle with anticipation, feel his breath warm against hers.

His eyes moved to the scoop neck of her top, noting the creaminess of her skin over the ripe soft curves of her breast, before moving back to her face.

The idea of seduction ran tantalisingly in his mind, just as it had done these last few months as he had drawn up the papers for her to sign. It would be good to possess her one more time, look down into her eyes as he enjoyed her. Then walk away without a backward glance, just as she had done, his papers signed.

It would be the ultimate retribution for the way she had so nonchalantly broken their bargain.

He looked into her eyes. They seemed incredibly blue, incredibly large for her small face. He bent closer.

'Jay, stop it.' Her voice was a whisper. There was no forceful rejection, just a husky, ragged plea.

It tore at his heart. He frowned, his hand dropping to his side as he moved back, the idea of retribution melting, like the snow outside on the pavement.

'Perhaps you're right.' He shrugged, his lips curving in a smile that didn't quite reach his eyes. 'Perhaps we should forget the past.'

She didn't answer.

'So, tell me, are you seeing someone else?' His bantering tone lashed against fragile senses.

'I don't really think that is any of your business, do you?' She tried to compose herself, tried to forget the sudden rush of need that had assailed her just moments ago.

'I'm just curious.'

'It's none of your business.' She flared again. She shook her head. How dared he come here with his divorce papers, and then bait her about old times, with that gleam of seductive charm in his eye? 'And let me tell you, Jay Hammond. If you came in here with any intentions of having a roll in the sack for old times' sake, then you can think again. I wouldn't want to go to bed with you if you were the last man left alive in the universe.'

He smiled. 'And this from the woman who was begging me to marry her just eighteen months ago.'

The mocking words made her temper rise even further. 'I didn't beg you to marry me.'

'Didn't you? Must have been some other raven haired beauty.'

'I suggested a business plan,' she murmured tightly.

'Ah, yes, the wonderful business plan, that you were deriding over dinner in holier than thou tones…it's all coming back to me.'

Her cheeks felt as if they were on fire, her blood racing wildly through her body. 'So, are you making business plans with anyone else?' he murmured derisively. 'Is that the question I should really be asking?'

'No! But I am seeing someone else. Someone very special.' She flung the words at him.

'Well, good for you.' In contrast to her he was perfectly cool. 'I hope you'll be very happy, Beth. All I ever wanted was for you to be happy.'

She wanted to say, Is that why you screwed your secretary behind my back? But she held her tongue, furious

with herself for losing her temper in the first place. She
would never lower herself to make a comment like that,
or show in any way that she cared one damn about his
affair.

Silence fell between them.

'You'd better go,' she told him heavily.

He nodded. 'I'll fetch your briefcase and drop it into the
office for you to pick up in the morning. If that's all right
with you?'

'Perfectly.'

She walked to the door with him. Now he was going
she wished even more that she hadn't lost her temper. And
what had been the point in lying about her private life?
He probably didn't give a damn who she was seeing, anyway. He wanted a divorce, for heaven's sake!

Pride, that was why she had lied, she told herself as she
watched him put on his coat. Pride had always been her
downfall. It was the reason she hadn't told him the truth
when she'd asked him to marry her; it was the reason she
hadn't told him the truth when she'd walked out on him.
It was a dreadful emotion, yet she couldn't help it.

She didn't want him to think she cared. And she didn't
want him to know that no one had taken his place, either
in her heart or her bed.

'Leave my briefcase at the reception area of my office
in the morning. I'll sign the papers and send them on to
you,' she told him stiffly.

'Okay. Goodnight, Beth.'

'Goodnight.' She watched as he walked towards his car,
got in and drove away. All that was left were the tyre
marks on the virgin white snow. Was that it? she asked
herself. The end of a marriage? The last time she would
ever see Jay Hammond?

She closed the door firmly and leaned back on it. I don't care, she told herself fiercely. But no matter how many times she said those words they still rang hollowly inside her.

CHAPTER THREE

JAY was caught up in the early-morning traffic when the phone rang. He frowned and looked around the car in some confusion. Where was that ringing coming from? He didn't have a mobile phone with him. It took him a moment to realise it was coming from Elizabeth's briefcase.

Checking in his mirror, he switched lanes and pulled to a standstill next to the kerb before opening the case to answer it.

Just as he got it out, it stopped. 'Damn things,' he muttered, and was about to put it away when it rang again.

He pressed the button and connected the call. 'Hi, it's Lucy.' A warm and very attractive voice said in his ear. 'We're still on for tonight, aren't we?'

'I don't know,' Jay drawled with amusement. 'That depends on where you are planning to take me?'

'Sorry.' There was confusion in the voice now. 'I seem to have the wrong number.'

'Are you looking for Elizabeth?' Jay asked.

'Yes.'

'Then you haven't got the wrong number, just the wrong person. I'm Jay...Elizabeth's husband.'

'Really?' The voice sounded alert and amazed now. 'Are you two getting back together? Gosh, that's so good to hear. I do like a happy ending. When did you arrive in London? Beth hasn't said a word.'

'Only yesterday—'

'Well, listen, I'm glad you've answered the phone,' she gushed on without pausing for breath. 'You know it's Beth's thirtieth birthday today?'

'Yes—'

'Well we're having a surprise party for her after work. It's at the Mayfair Tower Hotel. I'm calling for her at the office at six-thirty. She just thinks we're going for a few quiet drinks, so it's going to be a great surprise for her...well, I hope it is. She isn't suspicious, is she?'

'Not to my knowledge,' Jay said truthfully.

There was a moment's silence, a moment where Jay could almost hear the other woman's mind ticking over.

'Seeing as we are having this friendly chat, maybe you could tell me about the guy Beth is seeing,' Jay said nonchalantly.

'What guy?'

'She says she's seeing someone and it's quite serious.'

He heard the woman swallowing nervously at the other end of the line as she realised she had made a big mistake and a huge assumption. 'You're not getting back together, are you?'

'Not quite. But don't worry about it, Lucy.' Jay took pity on her. 'And your secret is safe with me. Thanks for the invitation, by the way.' Then he hung up.

For a moment he sat at the edge of the traffic and thought about things. Was there someone serious in Beth's life? Her friend hadn't seemed to know what he was talking about. On the other hand, she couldn't know much about Elizabeth if she could assume so easily, from him answering a phone, that they were back together.

Jay reached for a piece of paper and scribbled down the address she had given for the party tonight. Maybe he'd check it out.

'The report you wanted from Marketing.' Robert put the stack of papers down on top of the manila envelope. 'Cheer up, Elizabeth.' He leaned over and grinned at her. 'It might never happen.'

'I hate it when people say that,' Beth murmured.

'Yes, so do I,' Robert admitted with a laugh. 'Because it usually does happen…well, it does to me, anyhow.'

She smiled at him.

She'd always liked Rob. He was a couple of years younger than her, a pleasant guy, always helpful at work. He wasn't bad looking either, she supposed. Tall with dark hair that fell forward over his forehead like an absent-minded professor. She knew he liked her; it was obvious from the way he kept asking her out. But, although she thought he was a nice person, she didn't feel any attraction for him.

Maybe she should try and make herself feel an attraction. There hadn't been anyone in her life since she had left Jay. She needed to change that, get on with her life. Next time he asked her out, she'd accept, she thought suddenly.

But for the first time ever, Robert hurried away without issuing his usual invitation for a drink. She sighed. Maybe it was just as well. Getting involved with a work colleague could lead to complications.

She picked up the report he had left. Beneath it the manila envelope stared at her, heavily foreboding.

Jay had dropped her briefcase at the reception early this morning. Now it was late afternoon and she still hadn't got around to looking inside that envelope. Nor had she got around to having any lunch. The day was turning out to be even more hectic than usual.

Wonderful way to spend a birthday, Elizabeth thought as she rushed off to another meeting. Still, at least she could look forward to having a quiet drink with Lucy after work.

The last meeting of the day overshot and it was almost six-fifteen by the time Elizabeth managed to finish.

She raced to the cloakroom to freshen up. Changed out

of her work blouse into a sparkly halter neck top. Re-applied some deep red lipstick. Fluffed up her hair and then bent closer to the mirror to examine herself with a critical eye.

Not marvellous, but she'd do, she decided, putting on her black jacket. She picked up her bag with the divorce papers tucked safely inside and made her way out of the building. Nobody was around. Most people seemed to have left early today for some reason.

Lucy wasn't in the reception, but had left a message saying she was caught up at work; could they meet outside the Mayfair Tower Hotel?

Sounded as if Lucy's day had been as hectic as hers, Elizabeth thought as she hailed a taxi.

Lucy was waiting inside the foyer when Elizabeth arrived. She was twenty-nine, blonde and extremely attractive. She was also great fun. They had been friends ever since Beth had handled an advertising contract for Lucy's dating agency eight months ago.

'Happy birthday, you old codger!' she said now, reaching to kiss her.

'Wait until it's your turn.' Beth grinned.

'So how are you?' Lucy asked casually as they made their way through the busy foyer.

'Don't ask.'

'That good eh?' Lucy slanted a look over at her. 'Any news?'

Elizabeth shook her head. 'Apart from my husband asking me for a divorce, you mean?'

'Oh, hell!'

'Never mind. I'm over all that now.' Elizabeth smiled and linked her arm through her friend's. 'In fact I'm so over it that I'm going to buy all the drinks tonight by way of a celebration. What are we doing here, by the way?'

'Someone told me about a new bistro, so I thought we'd

try it.' Lucy explained airily as she led the way down a corridor.

Elizabeth frowned; she hadn't heard about a new bistro here.

'You're not setting me up on a blind date, are you?' she asked, suddenly very suspicious as they stopped outside one of the function suites.

'Would I do that to you?' Lucy teased, opening the door and stepping back for her to enter the room first.

'Yes—' Elizabeth walked into a darkened room with a frown.

'Surprise!'

Lights flooded over her and a chorus of voices sang 'Happy Birthday'. She looked around the room in a daze as her friends and work colleagues came across to slap her on the back.

Someone took her jacket; someone else pressed a drink into her hand.

'Many happy returns,' John, her boss, said with a grin. 'Sorry I worked you so hard today.'

'That's okay.' Elizabeth wasn't sure if she was pleased or horrified by all this fuss. She cringed as she saw the banner saying 'HAPPY 30' hanging over the table of food. She had been hoping to keep her birthday quiet.

'I'll kill you, Lucy,' she murmured to her friend, and then had to smile. 'But, thanks, anyway.'

Then she saw Jay standing at the far side of the room and her heart seemed to do a forward roll. He was standing slightly apart from the crowd. Two secretaries from her office were engaging him in conversation. He raised his glass to Elizabeth as their eyes met across the room.

'What's he doing here?' she asked, horrified.

'Who?' Lucy followed her gaze across the room.

'Jay,' Elizabeth enlightened her, then fixed her with a level stare.

'Oh, Beth!' Lucy looked truly horrified. 'I'm really sorry,' she hissed. 'I didn't think he'd come, not really—'

'He's coming over.' Beth downed the drink someone had given her in one gulp. It wasn't wine, it was some sort of punch and it tasted awful.

She noted the purposeful expression on Jay's face as he headed towards her. He wasn't going to ask her for those divorce papers, was he? she wondered in panic. Surely even Jay had more sensitivity than to do that at her birthday party.

'Happy birthday, Elizabeth.' He stopped next to her.

'Thanks.' She tried not to let her gaze wander over the expensive cut of his dark suit, the colourful tie. He looked good, she had to admit, somewhat grudgingly. But, then, he always looked good. 'At the risk of sounding rude, Jay, why on earth are you here?'

'Lucy invited me.' He slid a sideways glance at Lucy. Elizabeth was amazed to notice how her friend blushed as their eyes met. Another conquest, she thought dazedly. How and when had that happened?

'I presume you are Lucy?' he asked, dispelling the notion in Elizabeth's mind that they had already met.

'Yes, that's me.' Lucy gave an apologetic smile over at Elizabeth. 'I spoke to him by mistake on your mobile phone this morning.'

'Yes, we had quite a chat, didn't we?' Jay said with a grin.

'Would you like a glass of wine, Elizabeth?' Lucy asked, changing the subject and obviously desperate to get away.

As she disappeared amidst the crowd, Elizabeth trained her attention back on Jay. 'You've embarrassed her,' she accused coolly.

'Oh, come on, Beth. It's a sad situation if I can't come and wish you a happy birthday…don't you think?' he murmured. 'Anyway I didn't like the way we left things last night.'

'What way was that?' she asked innocently.

He smiled and his eyes moved over her slender figure. 'You might find this hard to believe, Beth, but I don't like being at loggerheads with you.'

'Don't you?' She shrugged. 'Well it doesn't much matter any more.'

'It matters to me,' he answered softly.

She felt a tremor of awareness race through her body. When he spoke like that, when he looked at her like that, she felt so confused. She battled against the feeling of weakness inside her, the voices that were reminding her how wonderful it had once been to be held in his arms, cradled close, kissed passionately.

'I've brought you a gift.' He handed her a small black jewellery case wrapped with a gold bow. 'Happy birthday.'

She stared at it suspiciously before looking up at him with narrowed blue eyes.

'Well, go on, open it.' He grinned. 'It's not a time bomb.'

She took it and, with hands that were none too steady, flicked back the gold bow and opened the case.

A topaz pendant on a fine gold chain stared up at her from the velvet box. It was a stunning piece of jewellery. One, judging from the name on the box, that he had obviously purchased in the Caribbean.

'It's beautiful.' She frowned, trying to make sense of this. 'But there was no need for it...' She snapped the lid shut on the gift. 'I've told you I'll sign the papers. So you can cut the phoney caring stuff.'

Before Jay could reply they were interrupted by Robert. He pushed a glass of champagne into Elizabeth's hand and reached to kiss her on the cheek. 'Happy birthday.'

'Thank you.' She smiled at the other man. She was

aware that he was looking at Jay now, waiting for an introduction. Before Elizabeth could say anything, Jay stretched out his hand. 'Hi, I'm Elizabeth's husband,' he said easily.

'Oh!' Robert stared at him for a moment, surprise clearly evident in his expression.

Elizabeth was taken aback as well. Uncertainty rushed through her. Why had Jay introduced himself like that? He might be her husband by law, but he certainly had no right to stake such a claim in public.

He smiled at her. It was the kind of smile that made butterflies dance in her stomach.

'You didn't tell me you were married, Beth.' Robert's voice broke the spell holding her, bringing her sharply back to reality.

'Didn't I?' She wrenched her eyes away from Jay, noticing the dismayed expression on Rob's face. Taking pity on him, she explained, 'Jay is soon to be my ex-husband.'

'Oh! I see.' Robert's face cleared. 'Well, it's good you can remain friends. Always the best solution, I think.'

'Do you?' Jay murmured, a hard edge to his tone. 'I suppose you are right.'

Elizabeth glanced back at him. The dark eyes looked cold now as they met hers. He looked angry, she thought and then wondered if she had imagined it as he smiled lightly.

Music started to boom from the speakers beside them as the DJ started the evening's entertainment.

The lights dimmed and coloured strobe lights swept around the room, giving the illusion of a dark, smoky nightclub.

'Come on, Elizabeth, come and dance,' someone urged.

She looked around and saw Lucy beckoning to her by the edge of the dance floor. Glad of the reprieve, she handed Jay his gift back and with a polite smile headed towards her friend.

'I'm really sorry, Beth.' Lucy had to shout over the music. 'But I honestly didn't think he'd come.'

'Doesn't matter, forget about it,' Elizabeth shouted back as she put her champagne down and followed her friend onto the dance floor.

Jay pocketed the gift again and watched Elizabeth from the shadows.

She'd lost weight since leaving him, he observed, his eyes moving over the long length of her legs in the black trousers to the silver of her top…a top that left little of her sensual curves to the imagination.

He felt desire stir within him, just as he had the moment he had seen her again at her office. She had always been an attractive woman, but now…now she took his breath away.

'So, who's the guy?' Ruth, one of the secretaries, who had been speaking to Jay earlier, caught up with Elizabeth on the dance floor. 'He's gorgeous.'

'Do you think so?' Elizabeth didn't need to ask who she was talking about.

'I think I've died and gone to heaven,' Ruth drooled. 'Listen, do you mind if I ask him out, or are you and he…?'

'No. Go ahead,' Beth told her airily, and watched as Ruth lost no time heading off in Jay's direction with a look of determination on her face.

The music changed and Lucy put her hand on Beth's arm. 'Shall we have another drink?'

'Why not?' Elizabeth shrugged, ignoring the warning bells inside her body. She still hadn't eaten so the few drinks were having more effect than normal. She could feel them working their way through her system, making everything distant and a little unreal.

She watched across the room as Ruth caught hold of Jay's arm and led him towards the dance floor.

'Does it bother you?' Lucy asked, following her gaze.

'No, of course not,' Elizabeth said brightly, too brightly, she feared, by the look of sympathy in her friend's eye.

'Why do you think he came here tonight?'

'Because you asked him?' Elizabeth ventured with a grin.

'Yes, but only because I thought you were back together…it was a misunderstanding. I didn't think in a million years he'd turn up tonight. I mean, it's not customary, is it, for an estranged husband to want to be at his ex's party?'

'Jay's never been one for observing social niceties,' Beth murmured. 'He probably thinks it's quite logical to come to my birthday party, and assumes that if he can keep things friendly I won't make the divorce difficult for him.'

'What happened between you two anyway?' Lucy asked curiously. 'You've never really talked about why the marriage broke up.'

Elizabeth hesitated.

'If you'd rather not tell me, I'll understand,' Lucy said quickly.

'No…it's all right.' Elizabeth shook her head. 'I'm over all that anyway.' Despite the words, her voice wasn't entirely steady. 'I caught him with his secretary. Apparently they had been having an affair for some time.'

'Ouch!' Lucy grimaced. 'I'm sorry, Beth. I shouldn't have asked.'

Elizabeth shrugged as if she couldn't care less. But, in truth, the memory of Lisa Cunningham entwined in Jay's arms, her lips pressed against his, still had the power to make her feel sick inside. 'Well…ours was never really a love-match in the first place.' She tried to lighten her tone.

'And at least I escaped with my pride intact. I was the one to finish with Jay. To this day he doesn't realise that I know about the affair, or that I saw them together.'

'So you managed to make a dent in his ego on your exit?' Lucy smiled. 'Good for you.'

'I don't think anybody could dent Jay's ego,' Elizabeth murmured.

'Hey, Beth would you like to dance?' Robert asked, sauntering over.

She was about to say no, until she noticed the way Jay was dancing with Ruth. Her arms were around his shoulders and he was holding her close. He'd got some nerve, she thought furiously, watching as he smiled down at the pretty blonde. Jay had always had a thing for blondes. Lisa was blonde.

'Elizabeth?'

She looked back at Robert and found herself smiling. 'Yes, why not?' she said blithely.

The evening seemed to pass in a blur of people wishing her well, asking her to dance. Even chauvinistic Colin asked her for a dance, and some guy she'd never met before who said he worked in Accounts. Then Robert again.

'I almost let the secret out today in the office,' he said smiling down at her. 'You looked sad and I wanted to say, Cheer up, nobody has forgotten your birthday—'

'Thanks, Rob.' She couldn't concentrate on what he was saying because suddenly over his shoulder she had noticed Jay talking to Colin and her boss at the bar.

'How about having dinner with me next week?' Robert asked suddenly.

'Yes, that would be nice,' Elizabeth murmured. She frowned as there was a guffaw of laughter from the bar. What were they talking about?

'Robert, would you mind if I sat down?' she asked suddenly, deciding to go over there and find out.

'No…of course not.'

'Thanks. See you later.' She pulled away from him and headed towards the bar.

Colin pulled a stool out next to him as he saw her approach. 'Really good party, Beth,' he said amiably. 'Can I buy you a drink?'

She looked at him in surprise. Colin the chauvinist was never usually so pleasant. She didn't really want anything else to drink, but to be sociable she thanked him and asked for a lemonade.

Her boss leaned over towards her. He was about fifty, with greying hair, which made him look distinguished. 'Jay's just been telling us about the yacht he is designing for the round-the-world race. It sounds quite revolutionary in terms of design.'

'Really?' She met Jay's eyes. 'How interesting,' she murmured dryly.

Unaware of the irony in her tone, John nodded with enthusiasm, then turned his attention back to Jay. 'As I was saying, if you are interested in some advertising to promote the yacht give me a call.'

'I will, John, thanks,' Jay said easily.

Elizabeth met Jay's eyes across the bar. If he wanted some advertising he could use another company, she thought. She certainly didn't want Jay coming round to the office.

He just smiled at her as if totally unaware of her displeasure.

'Well, I'd better make tracks,' John said, glancing at his watch. 'I told my wife I wouldn't be too late.'

'I'll give you a lift,' Colin offered, finishing his drink.

As the two men took their leave, Elizabeth was left with Jay, an empty bar stool separating them.

She glared over at him. 'Just what are you up to?'

'I don't know what you mean?' His dark eyes were full of innocent enquiry. But she wasn't fooled for a moment.

'Yes, you do.' She took a sip of her drink. 'You shouldn't have come here tonight. And what was all that rubbish about using our agency?'

'That was just something that cropped up in the conversation. It was Colin's suggestion.'

It would be, Elizabeth reflected furiously. Colin was always on the look-out to steal some kind of march on her. 'You're not seriously contemplating doing business with our agency, are you?'

'Why not?' Jay shrugged. 'Promoting the yacht might be good for the boat yard. Colin was suggesting making a short film of the vessel for the Earl's Court Boat Show.'

'You're here to get me to sign your papers,' Elizabeth rasped impatiently. 'Not to start an advertising contract.'

He shrugged. 'Why can't I do both?'

'Because I don't want you around for longer than is absolutely necessary,' she retorted quickly.

'That's not very friendly of you, Elizabeth,' he rebuked, a taunting note in his voice. 'Don't you think the least we can do is be civil to each other? After all, neither of us is really to blame that things didn't work out between us. Are we?'

She didn't answer.

'You didn't want to marry me, anyway; it was your father's wild idea. And it was your decision to leave. What was it you said? "I can't live a lie any longer'?''

She felt her heart thud heavily against her chest. That was exactly what she had said. She remembered the tightly controlled words, the look of surprise on his face.

'Let's face it,' she had said. 'This just isn't working out.'

'Isn't it?' he had said calmly. 'You've got a share in your father's business...isn't that what you wanted?'

'Can't we just be friends?' Jay asked her now, bringing her back to the present with a start.

'What's the point?' She looked away from him.

'I'm sure your father wouldn't have wanted us to end up enemies,' Jay said softly.

Her eyes glittered with unshed tears as she looked swiftly back at him. 'Don't bring my father into this,' she told him shakily.

'It's a bit late for that, isn't it?' Jay shrugged. 'He's the one who started all this.'

She didn't make any reply and he moved across into the stool next to her.

'You wouldn't have married me if he hadn't left his will like that. So you can't really blame me if the situation wasn't to your liking. I did try.'

'You did nicely out of the arrangement,' she answered quickly. 'You got an up-and-coming business and a partner who let you run it the way you wanted to.'

'Look, Beth. I've invested a lot in the business, not just time, but money as well. I could have done that with Cheryl as my partner right back at the beginning, I didn't have to marry you.'

'No, you didn't.' Beth looked away from him. 'But then, my stepmother might not have given you as much freedom with the business as I've given you.'

'Maybe not.' He shrugged. 'To be honest with you, Beth, I've always been wary of partnerships. That's why I wouldn't buy into the business years ago when your father offered to make me a partner.'

'So why did you go into partnership with me?'

'Well, you proposed a different kind of partnership, didn't you?' His voice was a husky drawl as he slanted her a teasing look. A look that for some reason sent a frisson of desire snaking through her body.

She tried to tell herself that the feeling was all in her

imagination, just as she had last night. But she knew deep down that she was lying to herself.

It was very perturbing to know that he could still turn her on. Just a glance, a smile, an intonation of his voice and her senses were flung into chaos. She should be immune to him by now, she told herself furiously.

'I went along with your game because I figured you deserved the yard, and I didn't agree with the way your father had left his will,' he continued after a moment's silence. 'Also, we were friends, and I thought an arranged marriage might just work between us. I'd fallen for fireworks and passion once before with my first marriage and that hadn't worked.'

She bit down hard on her lip. Willing herself not to care.

'Anyway, whatever the reason, I went along with your idea. Now you owe me.'

'I don't owe you anything.' She looked around at him then, her eyes wide.

'Oh, yes, you do.' He was quite calm. 'I've built the yard up into something very big. I've sent you very generous cheques at the end of every quarter. Now it's your turn to give something back.'

Her heart drummed fiercely against her chest. 'Like what?'

He shrugged. 'Well, you can at least be civil to me…and you can sign the papers I've had drawn up.'

'I've told you I'll sign them.'

'But you haven't done it yet, have you?'

Why hadn't she? The question blazed through her. Maybe she just didn't want to make things too easy for him…especially if he was going to marry Lisa. She wished she understood her emotions better where Jay was concerned. 'I can't believe you are hassling me about this at my birthday party,' she grated angrily.

'Neither can I,' he admitted ruefully.

She was surprised by the tone of his voice, the gentleness in his eyes. 'I didn't come here to hassle you, Beth,' he said softly. 'I came here because I want us to be friends. And I still care about you.'

She felt her heart miss a beat. He's full of hogwash, she told herself swiftly. Jay had always been able to charm his way out of anything...even a marriage.

The music was slowing as the evening was coming to an end. Jay looked past her towards the dance floor. 'Would you like to dance?' he asked suddenly.

'No, thank you.'

'Not even for old times' sake?'

'Definitely not for old times' sake,' she said fiercely, remembering their conversation last night.

He saw the glitter of defiance in her eyes and smiled. 'Okay, for new times' sake.' He reached and took hold of her hand. And before she knew what she was doing she was allowing him to lead her onto the dance floor.

This was crazy, she thought as he slipped his arms around her waist and pulled her closer. Absolutely crazy.

'It's about time I had a dance with the birthday girl,' he said, his voice close against her ear as he bent his head towards hers. 'Everyone else has.'

She allowed herself to lean against him. The familiar tang of his cologne sent a shiver racing down her spine. She felt his hand gentle against the naked skin of her back, felt his breath whisper-soft against her ear.

'I like dancing with you,' he said softly. 'I always did. Your body seems to fit so well against mine.'

Pull away, Elizabeth, she told herself distractedly. Don't let him charm you. He's a rat...a horrible rat, and you hate him.

Considering how much she hated him, it was strange how safe she felt in his arms. As if that was where she was meant to be. But, then, she had always felt like this around Jay. She felt the familiar surge of sensual need rush to life inside her, strong and sudden and totally over-whelming. She hated herself for feeling like this but she just couldn't seem to help it.

'I think I've had too much to drink,' she murmured. 'I feel kind of light-headed.'

'Do you?' His hand was gentle at her back. 'Shall I take you home?'

'No. I'll get a taxi.'

'What's the point in that when I've got a car outside?'

They were still swaying to the music and Elizabeth closed her eyes. 'I'll get a taxi,' she murmured again.

'Why? Will your boyfriend be jealous?'

She didn't answer that.

'Which one is he anyway?' Jay asked. 'I've been trying to work it out all evening.'

'None of your business.'

'I've ruled out Robert.'

'Why?' She tipped her head back to look at him. 'Let me tell you, Rob is a decent guy, kind and considerate. A better man than you'll ever be.'

'Really?' Jay grinned. 'But it's not him, is it? He's not your type.'

'How would you know what my type is?' she mur-mured.

He smiled. 'I think I'm more qualified than most on that particular subject. We did live as man and wife for six months.'

She felt herself blush under the steady, level gaze. Then she pulled away from him. It took a tremendous amount of will-power. 'I'm going to have to go home,' she mur-mured.

He nodded and watched as she walked away from him. Considering she had said that she'd had too much to drink, she seemed sober enough, she was walking in a straight line, she wasn't slurring her words at all.

Lucy was sitting in a corner talking to Robert. She went across towards them. 'I'm going home,' she said as Robert started to make some room for her at the table. 'I'll have to, I'm exhausted. But thanks for a lovely party.'

'Enjoy the rest of your evening,' Lucy said with a smile.

'What…reading my divorce papers?' Elizabeth grinned as she picked up her jacket and her bag. 'See you in the morning, Rob.'

It was cold outside. She put up her hand to hail a cab but it was busy and drove past her.

The snow from the previous night hadn't lasted, but it seemed to have brought in a touch of Siberia. She shivered in her flimsy jacket, wishing she'd worn her coat.

She was about to go back into the hotel to phone a cab when she saw Jay's car slowing down beside her at the kerb.

'I'm going your way, anyway,' he said, reaching across to open the passenger door.

She hesitated.

'Well, please yourself.' He shrugged indifferently and made to close the door again. She caught hold of it before it shut.

'You've persuaded me,' she said, getting into the warmth of the car.

'You always were damn awkward,' he murmured, but there was a gleam of amusement in his eye as he spoke.

'And you always were arrogantly irritating,' she retorted, leaning her head back against the seat. 'Where's Ruth, anyway? Shouldn't you have offered her a lift home?'

'Ruth who?'

'The woman you were dancing with earlier.'

'Oh…her. Man-eater extraordinaire.' He smiled.

'I thought that was the way you liked your women,' Elizabeth murmured, remembering Lisa. 'You've been out with quite a few man-eaters in your time.'

'Have I?' He sounded amused. 'Who?'

She wanted to say, Lisa Cunningham, for one. But she couldn't bring herself to even say the name. If he told her he was planning to marry her, she didn't know how she would react.

Her eyes moved over the handsome profile of his face. 'Do you remember that girl you were going out with the first time I met you?' she asked him suddenly.

He shook his head.

'Oh, you must remember her. She had a figure that would have rivalled Madonna in her superbra, and she tottered everywhere on impossibly high heels.'

'Sounds interesting.' Jay grinned. 'But I can't remember her. You must be going back...what, four years?'

Was it really four years since she had first met Jay Hammond? It seemed longer somehow, as if he had always been in her mind, in her heart.

'Yes...I suppose it would be four years ago,' she reflected. 'It was before Dad married Cheryl. He was spending a lot of time down at the boat yard. I used to worry about him.'

'He was a widower for a long time, wasn't he?'

Elizabeth nodded. Her mother had died when she was just a teenager. It had been a dreadful traffic accident on the Jamaican roads. Her father had been devastated and she had tried her best to look after him. One moment she had been a carefree teenager, the next a young woman, trying to run a house, trying to help him down at the boat yard.

'It's a good job he had the business. I think he would have really fallen to pieces after Mum's death if he hadn't had that to focus on.'

'He told me that you were the one who kept him together,' Jay said quietly. 'Said he wouldn't have got through it without your strength and determination.'

She had been strong for him, Elizabeth reflected. But it had been a front. Underneath she had been in pieces herself. 'That's a bit of an exaggeration,' she said lightly.

'I don't think so.' Jay shook his head. 'You are a very capable person. I know I've only known you in the last four years, but I used to watch you sometimes when you came into the yard at the weekends to help your dad. You always jollied him along. His desk would be in chaos, and he'd be in a black mood, but by the time you'd left he'd be laughing, and magically everything would be back in its rightful place.'

'He was a grouch sometimes, wasn't he?' Elizabeth smiled. 'But at least he had some years of happiness with Cheryl before he died.'

She fell silent.

Jay glanced across at her. In the glare of oncoming headlights her face seemed pale, her eyes shadowed. She was strong, so damn determined to be self-sufficient, not to need anyone, that sometimes he wanted to shake her. But there were moments, like now, when the mask seemed to slip. And he could glimpse the woman underneath, fragile, vulnerable and he wanted to take her into his arms.

'You still miss your dad, don't you?'

'Of course I do.' She took a deep breath and looked over at him, her eyes bright. 'But life goes on,' she said brightly.

'Yes…and once more the mask slips firmly into place.'

'What?' She frowned. 'What mask?'

'Never mind.' He shrugged. 'So…go on, then. Who was this woman you were reminding me about a few moments ago?' he said, bringing the conversation back. 'The one I was going out with when we first met.'

'I don't remember her name. I just remember Dad saying, "You must come down to the yard, Elizabeth, and meet my new boat designer, Jay. He's a really nice bloke and very talented." So I duly trotted down and there you were, with this gorgeous red-head draped over your desk in Dad's office.'

Jay laughed. 'Well, now you come to mention it, I do remember that... Sonia, I think she was called...or was that Olivia?'

Elizabeth rolled her eyes. 'She was sitting on your office desk and the kiss was so steamy that the windows were misting up.'

'Now you're exaggerating!' He laughed.

'No, I'm not, and I can't believe you can't remember her name...or maybe I can,' she added sardonically.

'Oh, come on, Elizabeth. It's a long time ago,' he said. Then, catching the teasing expression in her eye, he grinned. 'I can't be expected to remember all the women I dated at that time. There were quite a few. I'd just got a divorce, remember, and I was playing the field.'

He had certainly done that all right, Elizabeth thought, her light-hearted mood evaporating. He'd had one glamorous woman after another.

She turned away from his handsome profile and looked out at the darkened streets. She remembered the time he'd even asked her friend Joanne out, right in front of her at a dance. That had hurt.

One of her other friends, Dorothy, had caught the look of disappointment on her face. 'I wouldn't worry about it,' she had said with conviction. 'Jay is in stage one. It will pass.'

'Stage one of what?' she had asked, perplexed.

'Stage one of getting over his divorce. Which is to take every available woman out.'

'And what's stage two?' she had asked warily. 'Take every available woman to bed?'

Dorothy had grinned. 'Something like that. Take my advice and steer clear of that guy until he's got through at least stage five. It will take some time. He's been through a tough divorce, Beth. His wife ran off and left him for his best friend. That takes some getting over. Take it from someone who knows.'

So she had taken Dorothy's advice and settled for being his friend. He'd made a good friend too…she should have been content with that. Should have known her limitations. But, no, she'd had to push her luck. That was her problem: when she wanted something she couldn't take no for an answer; she had to pursue it. And her father's will had been the perfect excuse.

'Do you ever see your ex-wife, these days?' she asked Jay suddenly.

'No. Suzy is still living down by Port Antonio. But I heard that she has split up from David.'

'That's the guy she lived with after you split up; isn't it?' Elizabeth said warily. Although she had tried to draw Jay out on the subject of his first marriage many times, he had never talked much about it.

'Very diplomatically put,' Jay said with a grin. 'Yeah, David is the guy she left me for.' He glanced over at her. 'Why do you ask?'

'I was just curious.' She shrugged. She had always been curious about Jay's ex-wife. Interested to know the inside story of what had really happened between them. But she supposed she'd never know how Jay felt about his ex. He wasn't a man who liked to gossip. Maybe she should be relieved about that. It meant that if he ever remarried again, he wouldn't talk about her. She frowned. She didn't like the thought of Jay remarrying. In fact she distinctly hated it!

'Do you think the fact that you've been divorced once before makes it easier to go through a second time?' she asked him suddenly.

'You must be joking.' For a moment the raw note in Jay's voice was very evident. 'Getting a divorce from Suzy was one of the worst periods of my life.'

'You loved her very much, didn't you?' Elizabeth said gently.

'Once upon a time, yes.'

'You were probably still on the rebound from her when you married me,' she said in a matter-of-fact tone.

'I don't think so.' He frowned as he pulled the car up outside her apartment. 'Why are you asking me this now?'

'I don't know.' She shrugged. 'I've had a few drinks. It tends to make me maudlin.' She grinned at him, the look totally at odds with the words.

'Would you like to come in for a nightcap?' she found herself asking.

She saw the surprise in his eyes.

'I can sign those papers for you, and then you can get off,' she said.

'Fine.' He switched off the engine and they got out of the car.

So, why have you really invited him in? Elizabeth asked herself as she got her front door key out.

It was a mistake. And she was in no mood for signing those papers. In fact she was in a very strange mood. Confused...defiant...maybe even a little scared. She didn't understand what she was feeling. All she knew was that she didn't want to be left on her own just yet.

CHAPTER FOUR

THE central heating was on full blast in the apartment. The heat hit them as soon as they walked through the front door.

'You can tell you used to live in Jamaica,' Jay said, loosening his tie and taking off his jacket.

'I turned up the thermostat last night when it started to snow. I must have forgotten to turn it down again.' She threw her jacket over one of the chairs and then kicked off her shoes. 'Do you want to adjust it for me? It's on the wall outside the bathroom.'

Jay went to do as she asked. When he returned she had poured herself a lemonade. 'Would you like a whisky?' she asked, holding up the bottle.

'No, thanks.'

She sat down on the settee and curled her feet up underneath her.

'What's the matter?' she asked as he continued just to stand in the doorway, watching her.

'Nothing.' He shook his head. 'But I thought you said you'd had too much to drink already?'

'Jay, don't tell me what to do,' she said pointedly. 'And for your information I'm drinking lemonade. The whisky was for you.'

'Oh! Sorry.' He shrugged. 'I was only trying to save you a headache tomorrow.'

'I'll worry about tomorrow myself.'

She reached for her handbag, thinking how profound those words were. Once she signed these papers she would be completely on her own. All ties, all connections with her home in Jamaica would be gone. She frowned. No, that wasn't quite true. She'd still have a share in her father's business. Funny how she still thought of the boat yard as her father's. Even now, in her heart, it was his place, the place he had loved almost more than anything. When she closed her eyes and pictured her father, she saw him at the yard.

'Right, let's get the dreaded deed done,' she said with an over-bright smile.

She took out the manila envelope and slit the top of it open.

'Haven't you read the papers yet?' Jay asked with a frown.

'No.' She took them out, and put them down on the coffee table. 'Have you got a pen?'

'For heaven's sakes, Elizabeth, you've had them for two weeks and you haven't read them yet?'

She looked up at him with raised eyebrows. 'So what?'

'Well, for one thing you can't sign legal documents without reading them,' he grated impatiently.

'I'll read them now.' She picked them up and peered at them, but the black print seemed to blur against the white sheets. But it wasn't because she was drunk, it was because her eyes seemed to have misted with sudden tears.

She didn't want a divorce. She really, really didn't. What the hell was the matter with her, she wondered.

She glanced over at him, glad of the subdued lighting in the room. She couldn't bear for him to know that she was upset about this. Especially as he was so keen to finalise things.

'Do you think you could make me a coffee, while I try and wade through this?' she asked brightly.

'Sure.' He turned away into her kitchen. 'But I think it would be better if you read the papers in the morning,' he said sensibly.

She made a face at his retreating back. Then sighed and put the papers down. Her hand was shaking. She felt awful. He was probably right. She must just be overtired, she thought sensibly. Why else would she be so upset? Signing these papers was for the best. They didn't love each other, the relationship had been a mistake.

When he came back a few minutes later, carrying two cups of coffee, she'd pulled herself together.

'You okay?' he asked handing her the coffee.

'Of course I'm okay.' She took a few sips of the black strong liquid and grimaced. 'You make lousy coffee.'

'You're welcome,' he drawled sardonically. Instead of sitting on one of the chairs he moved the papers from the coffee table and sat down on it so that he was only inches away from her, his knees touching hers.

'I can't drink this.' She made to put the cup down, but he blocked her.

'Drink it,' he said sternly.

'You're a bully, do you know that?' she muttered, taking another sip. 'This is going to give me a worse headache than the alcohol.'

'I bet you were hard work as a child,' Jay reflected suddenly. 'Stubborn and rebellious.'

'I was an angel, actually,' she said, handing him back the empty cup.

'Looks of an angel, sting like a bee?' He smiled and put both of their cups down beside him.

'Do you feel better now?' he asked, his eyes moving gently over her face.

'I told you, I feel fine.'

'You look a bit pale.'

'Jay, cut the concern,' she said crisply, trying to ignore the gentleness of his tone, the dark sexy eyes. 'I don't need you to look after me.'

'You've made that more than clear,' he said softly. He

reached out a hand and touched the side of her face in a feather-light caress that sent tremors racing through her.

For a moment Elizabeth felt as if she was holding her breath. He seemed so very close to her. She noticed the way his gaze moved to where her top dipped between her breasts. The look sent a shiver of desire racing through her.

He leaned closer. She noticed the dark shadow along the firm jawline, the golden flecks in his dark hazel eyes, before her eyes locked on the sensual curve of his lips.

'So, which one of the men at the party tonight are you seeing socially?' he asked quietly.

'You've asked me that before and I gave you my answer,' she said. 'Why are you so interested?'

He shrugged. 'I don't know, maybe I want to check him out before I leave. Make sure he's worthy of you, that he'll look after you.'

'I don't need anyone to look after me,' she said quickly.

He smiled at that. 'Oh, Elizabeth…I know that,' he said shaking his head. 'Never before have I met a woman quite so determinedly independent and so sure of herself as you.'

She frowned. 'I'm not that sure of myself…you make me sound like some kind of rock, isolated and remote.'

'But you don't really need anyone, do you?' he persisted softly.

She looked into the darkness of his eyes and felt her heart turn over. She needed him, she thought suddenly. She wanted him. But he didn't love her. So what was the point?

His lips twisted wryly. 'I rest my case,' he said softly.

'I'm not always sure of myself,' she said swiftly. 'I am human, Jay. I have my insecurities like everyone else.'

'Go on, then.' He moved closer, his face seemed only inches from hers. 'What are they?'

'Well...' why did she feel as if he had backed her into some kind of corner... 'well...I worry about work.'

'Doesn't count,' Jay said, shaking his head.

She frowned. 'Of course it counts. Work is very highly pressured. I feel I've always got to be top, that the men who work alongside me are constantly watching, waiting for me to screw up.'

'But you never do, do you?'

'I have bad days.'

Jay shook his head. 'Those aren't insecurities; those are just everyday stresses of life.'

'They might be everyday stresses of life to you. But they are worrying.' She frowned. 'And I found a grey hair when I looked in the mirror this morning.'

Jay laughed. Then his gaze moved almost tenderly over her. 'Elizabeth, you have never looked more radiantly beautiful than you do at the moment,' he said huskily.

'I wasn't fishing for compliments.' Her voice sounded odd, just a gravelly whisper.

'I know you weren't.' The gleam of amusement faded from his eyes and he leaned closer. 'But I meant what I said.'

He was going to kiss her. She had a couple of seconds to assimilate the fact. Then, as his lips met hers, she felt herself dissolve inside.

She had forgotten how he could arouse her with just a kiss, forgotten how good his lips felt against hers. His hand traced softly over the naked skin of her back and with each kiss, with each caress, she felt little shudders of desire racing through her body.

She responded tentatively at first, her arms moving up and around his shoulders as if almost afraid to touch him.

One second she was telling herself to keep her distance, the next all barriers were swept away in a storm of longing.

The kiss deepened, became more frenzied.

'I want you, Elizabeth.' His breath was whisper-soft against her neck as his lips trailed a heated path down to her throat, kissing the pulse-points, his hands raking through her hair. 'I need you.'

Her heart was beating so fast against her ribcage that she felt it would burst, her mind was clouded with desire. She leaned back against the settee. Felt his hands against her breast, pulling at her clothing. Finding the lace of her bra and pulling that aside with an impatience that only increased her longing.

She wanted him too. Felt the need for him like a deep yearning ache. The kiss deepened, the touch of his hands against her body was exquisite torture. She wanted him closer. She wanted all of him.

His hands caressed her breasts, fondling her until she was breathless with need. Then she was allowing him to undress her, helping him as eagerness overtook all caution.

She wouldn't think about the rights and wrongs of this, she decided forcibly. She'd just enjoy it. Worry about the consequences tomorrow.

She was snuggled in against him on the cramped confines of the settee. He didn't want to move, but his arm was trapped and it was starting to go dead. He pulled it out from beneath her, but she didn't stir.

He smiled, his gaze moving over the naked, slender lines of her body curled against the white silk cushions.

She looked almost ethereally beautiful. He had loved her long dark hair, but he had to admit that the short, feathery style suited perfectly the well-defined shape of her head, and the lovely bone structure of her face.

Her lashes were long and dark against the pallor of her skin. She had perfect skin, satin smooth, soft and faintly flushed across the high cheekbones. Her rosebud lips curved slightly as if in wry amusement.

Her eyes flicked open, wide blue and, for a moment, vulnerable. The only time he'd ever got her to look at him like that was after they'd made love. It pulled some kind of string inside him, made him want to wrap her up in cotton wool, protect her...love her.

'Hi, there.' He kissed the tip of her nose.

'Hi.' She smiled sleepily and curled closer to him.

She hadn't woken up yet.

'Shall we make ourselves more comfortable in the other room?' He whispered the words against her ear and she smiled, putting her arms around his shoulders.

'I'm fine,' she murmured in sleep-laced tones.

'Maybe you are, but I'm not.' He pulled away from her a little, then scooped her up into his arms.

'Jay...what are you doing?' She awoke with a start as she found him carrying her with ease through to the bedroom.

'I told you, making myself more comfortable.' He threw back the covers on her bed with one hand and then lowered her down.

'Jay, I—'

Whatever she had been about to say was cut off by the urgent pressure of his lips against hers.

The sheets were cool against her back, his hands hot against her front. They curved around her breast, the thumb rough against the sensitised peak. Then his lips moved to where his hands played and she felt her breath drawn in on a gasp of desire.

Anything she might have said was forgotten as he moved over her. She felt the full length of his naked body pressing against her. Her hands trailed down over the powerful line of his shoulders, her nails digging into his back. Once more he moved inside her.

She gasped his name and then gasped again as he kissed

her, a sensual, drugging kiss that invaded her senses as he possessed her totally for the second time that night.

She shivered and kissed him back. Loving the feel of him against her. Loving him tenderly with a sweet submission so totally different from before, when she had fiercely met his demands with fiery need.

As the passion exploded inside her she clung to him, her arms tight against the warm moist body. She kissed his chest, it tasted salty. She nuzzled in against him. Her hands rubbed over the powerful shoulders, the tops of his arms. She had forgotten what a fabulous body he had, the sheer power of it, so masculine, so big, it made her feel small and secure and safe.

'Keep that up and I won't get any sleep at all tonight,' he murmured, moving inside her again. Thrusting deep, growling her name, kissing her lips with a savage passion that rasped against the softness of her skin in a strangely primal, very sensual way. She was breathless, she was dizzy as she moaned his name, her body moving instinctively in time with his, their bodies in perfect union.

When at last they reached the peak of longing, the peak of desire, the world seemed to slowly dissolve around her in tiny splintering pieces of glorious ecstasy.

'That was so…so good,' he murmured, nibbling her ear as they broke apart.

His breath against the sensitive skin of her neck tickled, and she smiled, curling in beside him. The sense of belonging was so strong. She didn't speak, just lay against him, listening to the sound of his heart beating.

She fell asleep in his arms. The most peaceful, the most blissful night of sleep she could remember in a long, long time.

When she woke up daylight was streaming into the room. She blinked against the glare, her hand searching the empty space beside her in the bed, before she realised that she was alone.

She sat up, holding the sheet firmly over her body. The room was empty.

'Jay?' Her voice seemed to echo in the emptiness of the room. She wondered if she was dreaming, or maybe she had dreamt last night. She turned to look at the alarm clock. It was seven-thirty. If she didn't get out of bed she was going to be late for work.

She swung her legs out from under the sheet. She felt achy, as if she had done a work-out in the gym. She also felt thirsty. She reached for the glass of water next to the clock and drank it down in one, long, thirsty swallow, wondering as she did so, where it had come from. She hadn't got herself a glass of water last night.

Then she saw the black jewellery box. She reached to pick it up from the table. Inside, the topaz pendant shone brilliantly in the early morning sun.

She snapped the box shut. Last night hadn't been a dream. God, what had she done? She frowned as fragments of memories started to flit through her mind. She hadn't been drunk—a little tipsy, perhaps. But she couldn't blame what had happened on alcohol. She'd been perfectly aware of what she was doing.

She put the jewellery box down and reached for her dressing gown.

'Jay?' she called tentatively as she walked through to the lounge. She saw her clothes scattered on the floor and cringed as she remembered the wild abandonment that had transpired in here last night.

One moment they had been talking, the next they had been devouring each other like two starving people ending a fast.

Her eyes moved from the clothing to the divorce papers which still sat on the coffee table. She groaned. Of all the crazy, wild things to do. They hadn't even used any contraception.

She sat down in a chair as her heart seemed to race a little too fast. She felt afraid for a second; then a ray of hope sprang from somewhere. Maybe last night had been a turning point. Maybe they would get back together.

She frowned. She had slept with him when they were married and it hadn't kept him faithful, or interested. What was different now?

'Big mistake, Elizabeth,' she murmured darkly. 'Big mistake.'

CHAPTER FIVE

'THANKS for a lovely party last night.' Elizabeth smiled brightly at her work colleagues as she walked through the office towards her desk.

'Didn't expect to see you until midday,' Colin murmured. 'By rights, you're supposed to get drunk on your birthday and have the next day off, aren't you? Not come waltzing in half an hour early.'

'I didn't realise, Colin.' She smiled at him. 'Maybe next year.'

Robert put her mail down on the desk. 'John wants to see you. And you've had two phone calls from...your husband.'

She straightened the piles of paper on her desk. 'Right, thanks.'

The phone had rung several times before she'd left her apartment this morning. She had known it would be Jay. But she wasn't ready to speak to him yet. 'Do me a favour, will you, Rob? If he phones again, tell him I'm in a meeting.'

'Okay.' Robert grinned at her. 'Are we still on for dinner next week?'

'Dinner?'

'You said last night...'

'Oh, yes.' She nodded, remembering. 'Dinner would be fine.'

'So what night can you make it? How about Tuesday?'

'Tuesday is great.'

Robert smiled and returned to his own desk.

Elizabeth turned on the voice-mail on her phone, and then headed for her boss's office.

John was on the phone when she walked in. She sat down in the seat opposite him and waited for him to finish, her eyes moving over the photographs on his desk. A wedding photo of him and his wife, and another of his two little girls.

He was a nice man, she thought idly, obviously devoted to his family. Would she ever have a family? she wondered suddenly. Or was she destined to be this sharp-shooting career girl all her life? Both would be good. But in her experience you never got it all...you were lucky to get one. She wished she knew where she was going with her life. Last night with Jay had just confused her further. She'd thought she was over him...now she didn't even know that for sure. The memory of his lips against hers, his arms tightly and protectively around her, made her ache inside with a kind of empty, hollow feeling that wouldn't go away.

'Now then, Beth.' John put down the phone and turned to her. 'I want to talk about this new account. We've had some problems with the figures. I think we need the accountants to—'

The phone rang again and he snatched it up. 'Yes. No. You deal with it.' He put the phone down again. 'Now, where was I?' He frowned and raked a hand through his grey hair.

'We were talking about the Menda accountant?' she offered helpfully.

'Yes...I—' The phone rang again.

'Sorry, about this but I'm expecting an important call.' He snatched it up. 'Yes? Well, do that, then.' He put the phone down again and sighed. 'Look, maybe we should talk about this over lunch. At least that way we'll kill two birds with one stone.'

Elizabeth nodded. Very often they would have a work-ing lunch together. 'Shall I book a table at Luigi's?'

'Yeah…' He glanced at his diary. 'One o' clock.'

When Elizabeth returned to her desk she had two mes-sages on her phone. Both were from Jay.

'Hi. Sorry I had to rush off this morning, I had some business I had to take care of,' he said nonchalantly. 'See you later.'

Elizabeth frowned. Was that an excuse? Maybe he was running scared in case she read too much into a one-night stand.

The second message was, 'Fancy a hair of the dog at lunch-time?' Then he'd left a telephone number and room extension. 'Phone me,' he'd finished. She had to smile. No, Jay never ran scared, she thought with a shake of her head. He'd probably thank her for last night, then casually ask if she had signed his divorce papers yet.

She wrote down the number. Then continued with work. She didn't want to phone him; she didn't know what to say. She wasn't sure if it was because she felt embarrassed about last night, or if it was deeper than that. She'd think about it later, she decided, punching out the number of the restaurant for lunch.

Jay waited a couple of hours for Elizabeth to return his phone messages. He tried to concentrate on some paper-work for the boat yard, but as the time passed he found it more and more difficult. He shouldn't have rushed off this morning. But he had been expecting a phone call from Lisa at nine so that she could fax through this paperwork. And Elizabeth had been sleeping so peacefully, he hadn't had the heart to disturb her. He frowned, picked up his car keys and decided to go and talk to her. He couldn't wait until lunch-time.

He sighed and put the papers back in his briefcase. He

couldn't concentrate. He hadn't meant to make love to Elizabeth last night. He'd wanted her all right, wanted her badly. But she'd had a few drinks and maybe, he'd taken advantage of the situation.

He parked the car in a car park near her office and walked the few blocks. It was a bright, sunny day, cold with a clear blue sky, the type of day he sometimes missed in the tropics. Fresh and invigorating, it reminded him of his home town in New England. He felt good. Maybe it was the sex last night, maybe it was the thought that he and Elizabeth were going to sort things out.

As Jay approached Elizabeth's office he saw her come out of the front entrance and turn away from him down the street. Looked as if his luck was in; she must be going for lunch, he thought with a smile as he quickened his pace to catch up with her.

It was only as she turned to go into the doorway of a restaurant that he noticed she wasn't on her own, she was with a man. Whether she had just met him at the doorway, or had left the offices with him, Jay wasn't sure.

The man turned to close the door behind him and he saw it was her boss, John. Elizabeth was smiling up at him, her hand on his arm, a look of warmth in her eyes.

Was something going on between them? Jay stopped in his tracks. She'd said she was dating someone and that it was serious. But, after the party, Jay had dismissed the words, thinking that if she was seeing someone it couldn't be that serious, because she hadn't seemed to be with any one man in particular. Now he wasn't so sure.

John was the only man she hadn't danced with last night. He was at least fifteen years older than Elizabeth. And, when he had left, hadn't he said something about getting home to his wife?

When he'd been wondering who Elizabeth's mystery man was, John hadn't even entered the equation. But maybe that was because John and Elizabeth were being clever…after all when you had an affair with a married man—your boss, to boot—you didn't conduct it in public or around members of staff.

For a wild moment he considered going into the restaurant and confronting them. Then he turned away. He had no right to confront them. He'd look like a jealous husband. He smiled grimly to himself and headed back to the car park.

When Elizabeth got home from work there were two messages on her answering machine. Both were from Lucy, wanting to know if she'd like to go out for a drink tonight.

She rang her back straight away. 'I can't, Lucy.' She hooked the phone under her ear as she reached for the papers on the coffee table. 'I've got paperwork to deal with.'

'Never mind,' Lucy said easily. 'How did you get on last night with your husband, by the way?'

'I think I made a terrible mistake…' Elizabeth trailed off as her eyes moved over the divorce papers. She couldn't work out what she was reading. 'Can I ring you back, Lucy?' she said hastily.

'You can't leave me hanging in suspense like this. What terrible mistake?'

'The age-old one. Sex.'

The doorbell rang as she started to read the papers again. 'Hold on, Luce…' She put the phone down and hurried to open it.

Jay stood outside. She felt her heart speed up as she met the darkness of his gaze, felt herself go warm inside as she remembered the passion of last night.

'Can I come in?' he asked after a few moments.

'Yes…of course.' She stood back hastily, realising that

she had been keeping him waiting. 'I'm just on the phone; I won't be a minute.'

She went across to pick up the receiver, conscious of him watching her from the other side of the room. She wished she had put on something more stylish this morning than the grey trouser suit and pink skinny-rib top. 'I'm going to have to phone you back,' she told Lucy. 'Sorry.'

'Is it him?' Lucy asked.

'Yes, I'll talk to you later.'

'Well, you haven't made too bad a mistake; he obviously wants you like crazy.'

Elizabeth glanced over at Jay. His dark eyes met hers coolly.

'I don't think so,' she murmured.

'Play hard to get, as if last night meant nothing. That always gets them more interested.' Lucy laughed. 'Speak to you soon.'

The silence in the room seemed very heavy after Lucy's cheerful tones.

It was probably a little late for playing hard to get, she thought wryly. But maybe Lucy was right, maybe she should play this cagily.

'You didn't return my calls,' he said.

'I'm sorry. I've been busy all day.'

'No time for lunch?'

She shook her head. 'I had to work through lunch.'

'They drive you very hard at that office, don't they?'

She wondered if she was imagining the cynicism in those words. She frowned. 'Well I suppose they do. I've only just got around to looking at these papers,' she told him lifting them up from the table. 'I—'

'Maybe we should discuss last night, Beth, before we talk about the papers.'

He took off his leather jacket and hung it over a chair. He was wearing a dark pair of chinos and a navy blue sweater. He looked handsome, so handsome that she wanted to forget everything and just say, Last night was wonderful. Maybe she should, maybe she should just forget stupid pride and see what happened.

'Where did you rush off to this morning in such a hurry?' she asked instead.

'I'm sorry about that. But Lisa had said she'd fax me some important document and—'

'Lisa?' She stared at him, her heart hammering feverishly.

'You remember Lisa, my secretary,' he said calmly.

'Yes, I remember her very well.' Elizabeth's tone was cold. Maybe she'd been in danger of forgetting Lisa a few moments ago when she had wanted to go into his arms. But now, with the merest mention of her name, the memories were disturbingly vivid.

'It was important, otherwise I'd never have rushed off like that.'

She shrugged. 'It doesn't matter, Jay. Really. You don't owe me anything... Last night was just one of those things.' She was damned if she was going to put her heart on the line now. She must have been mad to even contemplate it. 'I'd had a bit to drink and—'

'And you were feeling lonely?' His eyes narrowed.

She shrugged and sat down on the arm of the settee as her knees felt decidedly wobbly. 'Well, what's your excuse?' she asked, tipping her head to look up at him.

'I don't have one.'

'So, shall I just sign these papers and get things over with?'

'If you want.'

She frowned. She wanted him to tell her last night had been special, that it had meant something, but that was about as unrealistic as wishing she'd won the lottery when she hadn't bought a ticket.

She reached for a pen and tried to balance the papers on her knee.

'Are you on the pill?' Jay asked her suddenly.

'The pill?' She looked up at him, apprehension in her blue eyes.

'In case you'd forgotten, we didn't use any contraception last night.'

'I hadn't forgotten.' Her hands were trembling, and she had to put the pen down. She didn't want him to see that she wasn't in control of this situation. 'But I don't think that's any of your business.'

'Don't be damn ridiculous! Of course it's my business.'

'You didn't ask me about contraception last night…why should you today?'

'Well, last night things got a bit out of control, didn't they?' His voice softened. 'Look, Elizabeth, I'm not proud of the fact that I got carried away last night. But I want you to know that I care about you. And if something happens as a consequence, then I'll take responsibility—'

'Well…gee, thanks,' she grated sarcastically. 'But I don't want you to worry, okay?'

'So you are on the pill?' He sought clarification with a directness that made her cringe.

'No…I'm not.' She looked up at him with more than a spark of anger in her eyes. 'I live on my own, Jay, and before last night there was no earthly need for me to use round-the-clock contraception. Now, do you think we can change the subject?'

For a moment she thought he was going to question her further. But to her relief he left it.

She looked down at the papers in her lap. 'What's all this stuff about the price of the shares in the boat yard?' She couldn't believe she had been able to ask that question, and with such coolness, as if this was just business.

'That's the current market value.' His voice was equally

cool. 'If you flick over onto the next page, I've worked out projections for growth next year. So all in all I'm offering a very fair price.'

'Fair price?' She looked up at him, puzzled.

'For your share of the boat yard.'

'What's that to do with our divorce?' She was totally confused now.

'Not a lot. We need to sort the business out before we can think about divorce.'

The matter-of-fact tone made her look up at him sharply. The dark eyes seemed to drill right into her consciousness.

'You mean, these aren't divorce papers?'

'No. Was that what you were expecting?'

'Yes.'

'You sound disappointed.'

She felt her heart pounding against her chest. Disappointed was nowhere near what she was feeling. For a moment relief flooded through her, as if someone had handed her a reprieve from a death sentence.

Then, as his words slowly sank in, the feeling of optimism dulled. He didn't want a divorce…yet. He wanted the business side of things sorted out first. Nothing much had changed. He might not be asking for a divorce now, but these were the preliminary steps.

'I don't know how I'm feeling,' she answered honestly, a raw vulnerability in her voice.

'This has to be a first: Elizabeth admits she's unsure.'

'Are you being sarcastic?' she grated huskily.

'No, I'm not. You've got to admit, Elizabeth, you are usually very sure, very positive, about everything.'

She shook her head. She wanted to shout at him, she wanted to say, Don't you see? That's an act, that's not the real me, that's just the person I've had to become in order to survive. But she didn't say anything like that. She couldn't admit to him that she wasn't calm and confident and always totally in control. To let him know that would be to show weakness.

He came closer and sat down opposite to her on the arm of a chair. 'You should never have left Jamaica,' he said suddenly. 'Putting so much distance between us was a big mistake.'

'It felt like a good idea at the time,' she murmured, remembering how she had felt when she had discovered Lisa and Jay together, a confirmation of facts that had probably been staring her in the face for months.

'It made it virtually impossible to sort things out between us.'

'Things like the boat yard?'

'Well, I was thinking along more personal lines.' He shook his head. 'But, yes, okay, the boat yard.'

'And now you suddenly want to buy my half of the business,' she murmured. What for? So that Lisa can have it? The thought was horrifying. 'I don't want to sell my share in the business,' she said firmly, a hard certainty creeping into her tone.

He wondered if he had misread the expression in her voice a few moments ago. There was no hint of vulnerability in her tone now, she sounded brisk and businesslike. The light was fading in the room as it started to go dark outside. He reached to switch on a sidelamp, but it didn't help. Elizabeth looked up at him, coolly composed. He felt a pang of annoyance that he hadn't been able to pin her down at a moment when he just might have been able to reach her, get some straight answers.

'Why not?'

'Because I'm not ready to let go of it.'

His lips twisted wryly. 'Let's be sensible, Elizabeth. You're too far away to be able to have any real input in the business. And my hands are tied by having a business partner so far away. Anything I want to do has to be co-signed by you. That's a hell of a handicap.'

'Thanks,' she grated hoarsely.

'I'm not trying to be unkind, Beth,' he said gently. 'But in business terms you are a liability. I have ploughed a lot of profit back into expanding the business but to do more I need to take some business loans from the bank. They are willing, but they are concerned about your absence. They are the ones who have suggested that I buy you out.'

'Why should they be concerned about my absence?'

Jay shrugged. 'You know what banks are like: they want everything without any hint of risk. They see you as a loose cannon.'

'Very nice. Did you tell them that I only have the business's best interests at heart. That it had been my father's boat yard.'

'I don't think banks are very sentimental, Elizabeth,' he said with the first gleam of humour she had seen in him all evening.

'Well I'm not selling.' She put the papers down as if they were red-hot. 'You can go back and tell them the answer is no.'

'For heaven's sake, Beth. I've offered you a fair price—'

'I don't care. I won't sell.' Elizabeth got up from the arm of the chair and paced over towards the window, to stare out at the darkened London streets. 'You needn't worry. I'll go along with your plans for the yard. I won't hold you back. Whatever you want to do, I'll go along with it…within reason, of course. Just send me any papers and I'll sign them.'

'It's taken you two weeks to get around to even looking at these papers, Elizabeth. How the hell can I trust you to sign any other papers?'

'Because I've told you I will.'

'You told me you'd sign these.'

'Well, I didn't know what they were.'

'You told me you'd read them when we spoke on the phone.' He crossed over to stand behind her.

'No, I didn't.'

'Why won't you sell?' he asked her, his tone suddenly more reasoned, and calm.

'I told you, I'm not ready.'

'So your reasons are purely sentimental?'

'There's nothing wrong with being sentimental, Jay.' She turned around and looked at him then.

He was standing closer to her than she had realised and she found herself staring up into his eyes. Their bodies almost touching.

'No, there's not,' he agreed. The gentleness of his tone made her feel warm inside, made her long to put her arms around him, lean her head against his chest.

She took a hasty step backwards. 'That yard meant everything to my father. I can't just get rid of it on a sudden whim. I'll have to give it serious consideration.'

'Yes. I can understand that,' he said slowly, but he was wondering if there was more to it than that. Was her sentiment entirely to do with her father? Suddenly it occurred to him that if he could get her back to Jamaica, maybe he could find out. He stood little chance here; she was so wrapped up in work and there was the added complication of John. Maybe if he could get her on her own they could work things out.

He smiled, but it was a smile that lacked any humour. 'So what am I supposed to do in the meantime? Let the business dawdle in the slow lane?'

'No. I've told you I'll sign whatever you want—'

'That's not good enough. I've got three meetings with the bank next week. Things need to move forward swiftly.'

When she didn't say anything to that he continued

gently. 'Your father has been dead for over eighteen months, Beth. Maybe it's time to let go.'

'I've told you, I'm not ready,' she said, her voice so low it was almost a whisper.

'Then, you'll have to come back with me.'

She looked up at him, her eyes wide.

'It will only take up a few weeks of your time. You can sit in on the meetings with me, reassure my bank manager what a caring and supportive partner you are.'

'I can't come back. I've got work to see to.' She wondered if she sounded as panicky as she felt. The thought of going back to Jamaica scared the hell out of her. There were so many memories back there…so many ghosts that needed to be laid to rest—and she wasn't just thinking about her father, she was thinking about the failure of their marriage.

'You'll have to decide what's more important. Work here, or your business interests at home,' he said calmly.

When she didn't answer, he continued gently, 'Why don't you come back and see how you feel? Tell work you need a holiday…tell them you're ill, tell them your stepmother is getting remarried and you have to attend. Tell them anything, but stay for at least a couple of weeks and sort out your priorities.'

Still she made no reply.

'I need your help, Beth,' he said calmly. 'I bailed you out when you thought you weren't going to get the boat yard. Now, it's your turn to do something for me.'

She frowned. 'That's just not fair. I tried to help you with the business once before, Jay. When we were married, I offered to give up my job at Jewell Advertising and come into the office with you full time, but you turned me down—said, as I recall, that you didn't need me.'

'Well, I need you now,' he said calmly.

She faltered. A year ago she'd have given anything to hear those words.

'It's either that or let me buy you out.'

The words brought her back to reality with a snap. This was business, pure and simple. She shouldn't allow herself to be sidetracked. 'I'll think about it,' she said coolly. 'I'll have to ask John.'

She saw the look of annoyance on his features.

'I can't just walk out on him,' she said reasonably.

'Why not? You managed to walk out on me.'

She flushed. 'That was different.'

'Was it?' He shrugged, once more totally impassive. 'Please yourself. But my patience will only last so long, Elizabeth.'

'Is that some kind of a threat?'

'No. It's a promise. I can't function like this, Beth. You're driving me crazy.'

Elizabeth wished she had the courage to make a joke of that statement, say something flip like, You didn't complain last night. But she couldn't make fun of what they had shared last night...couldn't even think about it without the curl of longing and need flaring to life inside her. Don't think about it, she told herself crossly.

'We've got unfinished business...come home and sort it out. Otherwise I'll have to get solicitors onto it.'

Her eyebrows lifted at those blunt, no-nonsense words.

'I don't want to have to do that,' he said tersely. 'But I will if you force me.'

Then he turned away from her and lifted up his jacket. 'Ring me at the hotel tomorrow. I leave first thing Sunday morning, so don't take too long to get back to me.'

The decisive words rang in her ears long after he had closed the front door behind him.

CHAPTER SIX

SATURDAY morning, and without the distraction of work Elizabeth felt her apprehension returning. She rang Lucy to see what she thought about the situation.

'If someone told me I had to go to Jamaica I'd be off like a shot,' Lucy said immediately. 'Did you ask for time off at work?'

'Yes, I broached the subject with John yesterday. Said I'd got an unexpected invitation to a wedding in Jamaica. Which isn't so far from the truth. My stepmother is getting married again, Jay passed on her letter to me when we had dinner earlier this week.'

'And what did John say?'

'Surprisingly, he was very accommodating. Said I was due some holidays, that Colin would cover for me.'

'I bet that pleased you.' Lucy laughed.

'Pleased Colin even more,' Elizabeth said grimly. 'I can't help feeling I'm making a terrible mistake in going back.'

'If it's only for two weeks it can hardly hurt, can it?' Lucy said sensibly. 'Tell you what, let's meet up in town this afternoon, do some serious shopping. Get a wedding outfit that will knock Jay's socks off.'

Elizabeth grinned to herself as she put the phone down. Lucy was right. Two weeks in Jamaica was hardly going to radically change her life. She'd be able to see her stepmother, plus sort out the business with the yard. It was as good a time as any to go back.

The sensible words seemed to falter slightly as she phoned Jay.

'I'll book you on the flight with me tomorrow,' he said immediately.

'No—don't do that,' she said hastily. The thought of spending ten hours on a flight with Jay was making her instantly panic. 'I can't come straight away. I've got commitments at work to sort out before I can leave.'

'Okay. When are you planning on coming?

'Two weeks time. That way I can be there for Cheryl's wedding.'

'I was hoping you'd come sooner than that. I've got meetings lined up with the bank.'

'Well, can't you ring and reschedule them?' She remained firm.

'I suppose so.' He didn't sound impressed. 'Ring me once you've booked your flight, tell me when you'll be arriving,' he said. 'That way I can pick you up from the airport.'

'All right.' Her reply was hesitant. 'I'll phone you.' Did he expect her to stay with him? No…surely not. A hotel was the best option. She'd book one herself and then phone him from there. She'd go back on her terms and then everything would be all right.

Two weeks later, the confidence she had felt whilst taking that decision in London seemed to have deserted her.

She leaned against the rail of her veranda and breathed in the heady scent of tropical flowers from the garden. The midday sun was blistering. Nothing moved apart from the Caribbean Sea as it rolled against the palm-lined beach at the bottom of the hotel's garden.

Her eyes moved to the path that meandered from the main body of the hotel through to these individual beach bungalows. She had been watching that path for the last hour, sure that he would come soon.

A black cat lay curled asleep in the shade of a tree. Beth

wished that she could sleep in the shade, relax and pretend that she was here on holiday. But this wasn't a holiday, and she didn't think she had ever felt so tense in all her life. She walked along the veranda, her heels clicking on the marble floor.

The cat raised her head and looked over, reproach glimmering in the golden eyes at being so rudely disturbed. The colour of those eyes reminded Beth of the topaz pendant Jay had bought her for her birthday. And that in turn led her to remember their night of passion.

It was almost three weeks since she had slept with him. And here she was, back home again...or rather in the hotel further down the road from what had been home. Life seemed to be taking some very bizarre twists and turns.

She glanced at her watch and then moved out of the burning rays of the sun, back to the wicker chair. Jay was late... She wasn't going to look as if she was waiting for him, as if she cared or even noticed the time. When he deigned to arrive, she would be nonchalant. She would look up at him and say coolly, Oh, it's you, as if he wasn't her husband, just someone she had met briefly and couldn't remember his name.

She smiled with satisfaction at the thought and picked up the book she had been trying to read on the long plane journey yesterday. Ten hours from London and she was still only on page two. The words danced mockingly in front of her and then, like last night, she read the same line over and over. She couldn't concentrate.

When she had phoned Jay from the hotel late last night, he had sounded annoyed.

'I thought you said you'd phone me when you had booked your flight,' he had grated impatiently. 'I said I'd pick you up.'

'I know what you said. But I'm here now,' she had replied calmly.

She didn't want to rely on him, or be beholden to him in any way. It felt better like this.

'Must be a good book...' Jay's droll voice from beside her took her totally by surprise. 'Is it the reason you couldn't pick up the phone and get me to collect you from the airport?'

The book slipped from her fingers, falling on the floor with a sharp crack.

She looked up. He was leaning against the rail of the veranda, looking tanned, relaxed and incredibly handsome.

'Hello, Jay.' Her plans to be aloof and cool deserted her. All she could think was that she had missed him these last couple of weeks. When he had left London, she had thought that she would heave a sigh of relief, but she hadn't. Strangely she had missed the excitement, the adrenalin he stirred within her.

Something about the way he looked at her now made her heart stand still. Suddenly she longed for him to tell her he'd missed her. But that was crazy. They had been separated for over a year. Why should he suddenly start missing her now?

All he needed from her was her presence at business meetings and her signature on papers, nothing more.

'So, why didn't you ring me?' he asked again, coming around to sit opposite to her.

She watched as he settled himself in the wicker chair. He was wearing beige chinos and an open necked cream shirt. They suited him. He looked healthy, sensual. Her mind veered away from the word 'virile'.

Hastily she reapplied herself to the conversation. 'I didn't get a chance. I've been so tied up with work. It's taken quite a bit of rescheduling and reorganising to get two weeks off.'

'Working you night and day, are they?' he asked dryly.

'I've been busy...okay?' she said crossly. Why did he

always make her feel so defensive? She would have given anything at this minute for him to reach over and at least kiss her on the cheek. Tell her it was good to see her. But no, here they were snapping warily at each other again, like a couple of terriers protecting their territory.

His eyes flicked over the blue sundress she was wearing. She looked incredibly beautiful, cool and composed, and that irritated him, for some reason.

He glanced at his watch. 'Anyway, we can discuss what you've been up to at a later date. You better get your things together and we'll go.'

'Go where?' Beth asked cautiously, taken aback by the statement.

'Home, of course.' He looked at her with a frown. 'Where do you think?'

'Home?' She stared at him blankly.

'Well, you weren't thinking of staying here, were you?' He looked amazed at the mere suggestion, as if the thought hadn't even occurred to him until this very minute.

'Of course I'm staying here. That's why I've booked myself in for two weeks.'

Jay pursed his lips. 'Are you frightened of me?' he asked suddenly.

'Of course I'm not!' Her eyes widened. 'What an absurd suggestion!'

'So why choose to stay in a hotel when I have a house with four bedrooms?'

'Because...' When he put it like that, she couldn't think of a rational answer. 'Because it's not on. You and I are separated and—'

'And what? Your boyfriend wouldn't approve? Is he the jealous type?'

'My boyfriend?' She couldn't think what he was talking about for a second, then she remembered her little white lie. 'Oh...no, of course he's not jealous. He trusts me implicitly.' As she met the darkness of his eyes she felt compelled to take the lie even further. Though she couldn't for the life of her figure out why. Maybe it was to prove to him just how unafraid she was. 'He knows that whatever was between us is over.'

'Really?'

Jay leaned forward suddenly. 'You told him about our night of unbridled passion, I take it?'

The question made her temperature soar. She felt her face go bright pink, felt her body burn. She hated it when Jay was so damn forthright. Did he have no sensitivity whatsoever?

'It's those kind of remarks that reassure me I've made the right decision staying here,' she replied, and wished she didn't sound quite so prim and proper, that she could just smile and shrug that episode off.

'Frightened I might tempt you to a repeat performance?' He grinned. 'No, wait a minute…sorry, I forgot. You're the woman who wouldn't sleep with me if I was the last man left in the universe.'

She tried very hard not to blush further. She remembered saying those words and felt deeply embarrassed. Were they the reason he had taken her to bed, to prove her wrong? She wished suddenly that she was a million miles away from here.

And to think that her heart had leapt at the sight of him a few moments ago… She had actually imagined she'd missed him! She was going crazy. He was the most irritating, the most hateful man.

'Another reason why I booked myself into this hotel,' she said tersely.

He smiled. 'It's nice to know I can still get under your skin,' he said gently. The sarcasm had gone from his voice now and the eyes that moved over her were gentle. 'I shouldn't tease you…I'm sorry.'

'No, you shouldn't.' She felt confused now. She hated it when he was nice to her. It occurred to her that Jay couldn't really win. She hated him when he was taunting her, hated him when he was nice. But at least she was never bored around him.

She remembered her dinner with Robert a few weeks ago. It had been painful. No sparks, no attraction. When he had reached to kiss her goodnight she had felt herself freezing, and had given him a peck on the cheek.

'And, while we are on apologies, I've got another one to make,' Jay continued swiftly.

She stared at him suspiciously.

'I've checked out for you at Reception and settled your account.'

'What?' She glared at him. 'How dare you do that without at least consulting me?'

'I know...' He shook his head. 'Really it just never occurred to me that you wouldn't want to stay at the cottage...I was trying to be hospitable.'

'You were trying to be high-handed and arrogant,' she corrected. 'Well, anyway, I'll tell them you've made a mistake. That I still want the room.'

Jay grimaced. 'They've re-booked it already. They've got a delegation of people arriving for a conference. I think they were quite pleased when I said you were checking out.'

'Oh, for heaven's sakes!' Elizabeth glared at him.

'Don't look at me like that.' He grinned. 'I didn't do it on purpose. Look, pack your things up, come home with me and, if you're not happy, I'll flick through the directory and find you another hotel. How's that?'

She didn't answer. The thought of going home was making her heart beat unevenly. She felt as if she was being drawn into something that was out of her control and she hated to feel like that. She was at her most confident when she was calling the shots.

'So, what do you say?' He glanced at his watch. 'I don't want to hurry you, but I've got some business to deal with this afternoon at the yard.'

It was laughable, really, she thought. When had she ever been able to call the shots around Jay? Every time she had tried, it had ended in disaster.

'I'm not staying at the cottage,' she said getting up from her chair. 'At least, not for long.'

'Whatever.' Jay shrugged and got to his feet. 'Come on, get your things together. I haven't got all day.'

He stood silently in the doorway of her room, watching as she opened up her suitcase and started to throw things in. Beth wished he would wait outside. She needed to think about this situation and she couldn't do that with him watching her every move.

The shrill ring of his mobile telephone shattered the silence making her jump.

'Jay Hammond speaking,' Jay's voice was crisp and businesslike as he answered the call, but after a few seconds when he recognised whoever was on the other end of the line, he laughed and his voice relaxed. 'How are things this afternoon? Really?' Again that deep laugh that was somehow so sexy and provocative that Beth could feel herself tighten in response.

'Okay, I'll see you later. No, I've got some business to attend to.' His dark eyes flicked over towards Beth as she struggled to fasten the straps on her case.

'No, I suppose it will be later than that, but I can't really talk now. Yes, we'll do that. I'll see you later. Bye, Caroline.'

Who was Caroline? Beth wondered. Someone close to him, judging by his tone of voice. So where did she fit in with the grand scheme of things? What about Lisa?

He came across as she started to lift the suitcase down off the bed. 'Have you got everything?'

'Yes. I hadn't unpacked much last night.' She let go of the handle as he reached to take it from her, not daring to risk any contact with him whatsoever. It was crazy, but his close proximity did make her nervous.

She followed him outside into the heat of the sun, then through the reception area. She couldn't believe that he had checked her out of here, after all her careful planning! Of all the damn arrogant, irritating things to do, she told herself furiously as they headed out towards the car park. He didn't give a damn about protocol. Didn't care what she thought about him. Just went ahead and did his own thing, as usual.

He slung her case into the back of an old army Jeep and then opened the passenger door for her. Even though he had parked in the shade of a tree, it was boiling hot inside the car. She wound down the window and gulped for cooler air as she waited for him to get into the driving seat.

'I'd forgotten how hot it is in Jamaica,' she murmured as he started the engine. She suddenly felt sick. Whether it was the heat, or jet lag, or just the nervous anticipation of going back to Sugar Cane Bay, she didn't know.

He glanced over at her. 'It will be okay once the air-conditioning gets going.' His voice was surprisingly gentle. She wondered if she looked as ill as she felt. 'Wind up your window and I'll put the vents on full-blast.'

She stared out at the passing scenery, but was more aware of Jay's body close beside her than anything outside the vehicle. She noticed his hands on the wheel, strong, capable. She remembered how they had felt against her body, caressing her, arousing her towards ecstasy. The memory made her angry. She didn't want to think about things like that. That part of their life was over.

Yet here she was, going back to his house, the house they had shared as man and wife.

She wondered if much had changed there since she had left. She had made a few alterations when she had moved in as his wife. Little touches that had transformed it from the bachelor pad it had once been into a home. She closed her eyes and thought about the house, mentally moving from room to room, something she had done a lot when she had felt homesick in London.

'Feeling better?' Jay's voice interrupted her thoughts.

'Yes, thanks.' The car had cooled down and she did feel a little better.

'You look a bit pale.' He flicked another glance across at her. 'You'll have to lie in the sun for a while, see if you can get some colour.'

'I'm not here on holiday, Jay. This is strictly business.'

'There's nothing to stop you relaxing for a while, though. I only need you to go to a few meetings with the bank,' Jay said easily.

Beth frowned. She wanted to keep busy. 'Yes but I'll want to come into the yard, of course. Have a look at the books, see how things are going.'

'Of course.' Jay was relaxed and nonchalant. 'I'll be happy to take you into the yard, but not today. You should rest after that long flight. Take your book into the garden.'

'I don't want to rest,' she said firmly.

'It's entirely up to you.' He shrugged.

There was silence between them for a while, as he negotiated the twisty, potholed roads.

She looked out at the green fields, the distant blue mountains. Heat shimmered in a haze over the road in front.

They passed the turning that led up to her father's old house. Elizabeth strained her eyes to see if she could catch a glimpse of the old colonial-style building where she had been brought up, but it was well screened from the road by palm trees.

'It's probably just as well you can't see it,' Jay remarked suddenly as he caught the direction of her gaze. 'The house has fallen into disrepair since Cheryl sold it.'

'That's a shame.' Elizabeth shook her head. 'It was a lovely home.'

She leaned her head back against the seat and tried not to think about past times, about her father. Why did things have to change?

Jay reached over and took hold of her hand, giving it a gentle squeeze. 'He had a good life, Elizabeth,' he said. 'He had happiness with your mother and then later with Cheryl. Some people never have one real love in their life, he was lucky enough to have two. Don't be too sad for him.'

'I know…' Her eyes moved to the hand on hers, the touch of his skin against hers stirring a rush of longing.

She remembered how supportive he had been when her father had died. What a good friend he had been to her. Had she been so terribly wrong to want more?

Jay had never really wanted her. Their marriage had been a charade…a charade of her own making. It was that knowledge that had always helped her keep her pride and her dignity and had stopped her many a time from flinging bitter accusation at him about Lisa.

She supposed if she was a decent person she would let go of Jay now, allow him to buy her share of the boat yard. Speed the way towards a divorce.

Her heart thumped painfully against her chest. She pulled her hand away from his.

'I rang Cheryl last week,' she said brightly, trying to turn her mind away from divorce.

'So you did have some time in your busy schedule for a phone call,' Jay remarked dryly.

'Well, I didn't have time to write and she had sent that lovely letter to us.'

He nodded. 'She seems very happy, doesn't she?'

'Yes…I'm glad for her.' Elizabeth nodded. 'She was shocked when I told her we had separated. It made me feel guilty that I didn't write and tell her.'

'Maybe it was kinder not to say anything. The last thing she needed after your father died was more bad news,' Jay said gently.

'Yes.' Elizabeth nodded. 'And she was ecstatic when I told her we would come to the wedding.'

'You told her I was able to attend, did you?' Jay slanted a wry look at her.

'Well, yes…' Elizabeth frowned. 'Can't you make it?'

He nodded. 'Yes. I can make it.'

'So, why are you looking at me like that?'

He smiled. 'You accused me this morning of being high-handed. Checking you out of your hotel room without consulting you. But you're not so different.'

'Yes, I am. This is entirely different,' she maintained stubbornly.

The dark eyes glimmered with amusement. 'Well, you didn't consult me.'

'It's still not as bad as checking someone out of their hotel room.'

The car crunched over gravel as he turned it down the drive that led to his house.

'You're better off here. Besides, I had to bring you home. May would never have forgiven me if I'd left you at a hotel.'

'How is May?' Elizabeth smiled when she thought of Jay's housekeeper, a delightful woman with a broad smile and a motherly way. Elizabeth had always got on extremely well with her.

'Same as ever. Her son got married just after you left, and she's expecting her second grandchild now.'

'Goodness! Sounds as if her daughter-in-law's going to have her hands very full.'

Elizabeth was distracted as the house came into view.

It looked picture-postcard perfect. A white sprawling house built on the edge of the cliffs overlooking the Caribbean.

Legend had it that it had been a pirate's cottage at one time. He must have been a very successful pirate, Beth had once remarked to Jay and he had laughed. But there was no denying that this was a most spectacular house, with uninterrupted views from most of the windows right across the bay. Some steps at one side led down to the private white beach fringed with palm trees.

A sign hanging from the branch of an Australian pine proclaimed that this was Sugar Cane Cottage. Home! She was home.

Jay parked the Jeep under the carport and they stepped out into the heat of the day.

The air was scented with the salt of the sea, a few birds circled above in the clear blue sky. Turkey vultures, large and ominous, waiting and watching.

It was as if she had never been away, she thought as she walked around to the front of the house. She noted that the garden had been carefully tended, the flowers and trees she had planted were well-established now, giving a cottage feel to the garden.

Jay followed her, carrying her suitcase. 'May's son, Jake, has looked after the garden,' he said as he noticed her interest in it.

'He's done a good job.' She followed him into the hallway of the house. It smelt of lavender polish. The wooden floors gleamed in the sunlight that streamed through from the lounge. She glanced through the doors noting how elegant the room looked, with its chintz chairs and Indian rugs.

'Where is May?'

'She's had to take her daughter-in-law into town. Otherwise she would have been here to greet you.' Jay led the way upstairs.

It felt so strange being back, walking along the familiar corridors towards the master bedroom.

She had thought Jay would show her into one of the spare rooms, she was very surprised when he opened the door of the master bedroom...the room they had once shared.

'I...I don't want to sleep in here,' she said hastily.

'Why not?'

'Well, it's your room.'

Jay looked around at her, a glimmer of mischief in his eyes as they met hers. 'Frightened you might have to share?'

Despite her every effort she felt her cheeks flood with colour, felt her body tense. 'I just don't want to put you out.'

He smiled. 'You're not putting me out.' He put down her suitcase and stepped across to pull back the shutters that closed out the intense heat of the afternoon.

Sunlight fell across the huge four-poster bed with its dark baroque posts. It was covered with a heavy white brocade cover and delicately embroidered cushions, some of which had been wedding presents from friends at the yard.

A bouquet of tropical flowers adorned the dressing table, some photographs of their wedding next to it. Everything seemed just as she had left it. Even the few belongings she had left behind were still there, her silver hairbrush and some of her jewellery sat on the polished wood of the table. Her books were on the shelf beneath the window; some of them were ones she had had as a child.

'I don't use this room any more,' Jay said as he watched her look around.

'I thought you would have cleared my things out of here long ago,' she remarked.

'I wasn't sure whether you still wanted them. You can go through them while you're here and decide what you want to take.'

'Fine.' Her fingers traced lightly over the satinwood furniture. 'So where are you sleeping?'

'The bedroom next door. I moved there when you moved out.'

'Why?'

He shrugged. 'I never did like this room anyway.'

'Didn't you?' She frowned, wondering why. She thought it a most pleasing room.

He glanced at his watch. 'I'm going to have to dash off, Beth. We're expecting a delivery at the boat yard and I need to check it. We'll talk later, over dinner, okay?'

She was a bit taken aback by the fact that they would be having dinner together, but then they were living in the same house, so she supposed it was to be expected.

'Unpack. Help yourself to anything you want.'

'Make myself at home, you mean?' she quipped lightly.

'Yes.' He smiled at her. 'Make yourself at home.'

Beth looked into his eyes and suddenly she wanted to go into his arms. The need to be close to him, to have him hold her, was like a dull ache eating away inside her. She turned away from him.

'Okay, but I really can't stay here for very long,' she murmured apprehensively. 'I'll have to find another hotel.'

'Well, there's no shortage of hotels on the island,' Jay said with a shrug. 'We'll talk about it later.'

CHAPTER SEVEN

IT WAS surprising how quickly the afternoon passed once Jay had left her.

As she unpacked she discovered clothes in the back of the wardrobes that she had forgotten about. Beautiful designer dresses that were well cut and designed to get a woman noticed. She pulled them out, holding them in front of her and looking in the mirror. Remembering each one as if they were old friends, and recalling the occasions she had worn them. Some brought back happy memories, others, like the long black strapless dress, made her wince.

She had been wearing that dress the night she had discovered Jay was cheating on her. They'd been at a function at the polo club and she'd overheard the conversation in the ladies' room. From that time on, everything had changed.

'I think I've fallen in love,' the woman had said dreamily. 'No one has ever turned me on the way he does. Sex is just incredible.'

Elizabeth had recognised the voice immediately. She'd heard it often enough over the phone. It had been Jay's secretary, Lisa.

'And does Jay feel the same way?' her companion had asked.

'I don't know. All I do know is that he doesn't love his wife. Well, she's hardly in his league, is she? She's a bit of a plain Jane.'

'Which one is his wife?'

'Long dark hair, a bit on the weighty side. She's called Beth.'

'Oh, I didn't realise she was his wife.'

'Well, they've only been married for about six months.'

'Six months! They should still be on their honeymoon.'

'Yes, I suppose so, but he's not happy. Well, he can't be, can he? Otherwise he wouldn't be playing away. That marriage is just a sham. Jay probably got a tax break or something by marrying her. He's very well off in his own right and I suppose so is she. These moneyed types usually stick together, don't they?'

'So you don't think he'll leave her, then?'

Lisa had laughed at that. 'It's all very well Jay being pragmatic about a relationship in theory; it's quite another putting it into practice. He's a hot-blooded, passionate guy. I think he will leave her, if not for me then someone else. It's just a matter of time.'

Beth put the black dress down on the chair, trying to close out the memories. She stared at her reflection in the mirror, remembering the shock. She'd felt numb for days, too upset to feel anger, too upset even to cry. Behind her, the reflection of the huge double bed mocked her. She had continued to sleep with Jay for a while after that, but she hadn't been able to stand for him to touch her. She'd frozen when he had come too near. And yet she'd still wanted him, and that had torn her in two.

Then had come the evening when he had been very late home. He'd been working long hours at the yard, but eleven-thirty had been pushing it, even for him.

She'd got into her car and had driven over there. She hadn't stopped to think what she would do if she caught them in the act…instead she had prayed that Lisa had been making the whole thing up, that Jay would be sitting behind his desk, working alone.

How naive!

She'd seen them from downstairs in the yard. The light had been on in the office and Lisa had been sitting on his desk. As she'd watched, the woman had leaned forward and had kissed him, a smouldering, passionate kiss.

She had stood still for a few moments on the step, then she had turned away, confrontation too humiliating to contend with. Besides, all she had wanted to do was run away.

There had been no alternative. She'd had to leave, salvage the little pride she had left. But it had been the hardest thing she had ever had to do in her life.

The sound of the front door closing startled her out of her reverie. She glanced at her watch. it was nearing six o clock. Unless Jay had changed his working habits, it wouldn't be him.

She put the clothes away in the wardrobe and, with a quick check on her appearance, she stepped out of the bedroom.

She made her way downstairs just as the grandfather clock in the hall struck six.

'Elizabeth! How lovely to see you.' Jay's housekeeper came bustling out from the lounge, a welcome smile on her plump face.

'Hello, May.' She felt the tension easing inside at the warmth of the greeting.

'My heaven's, girl, what have you done to yourself?' May said as she looked her up and down. 'You've gone so thin!'

'It's nice of you to say so.'

'It wasn't meant as a compliment.' May's eyes were gleaming with merriment. 'You need feeding up! London certainly hasn't agreed with you.'

Elizabeth grinned. 'It's because I've been missing your home cooked meals.'

May looked delighted at that comment. 'I'm cooking something special tonight…a welcome home meal.'

'Thank you, May, that's really very sweet of you.' Elizabeth was touched by the gesture. 'What's this I hear about you being a grandma now?' She detained the woman as she made to move away.

'Yes, I've a grandson, Paul. He's just three months. And Erica is expecting again. So it's all very exciting.'

'That's lovely, May. You must be so thrilled.'

'I am. And I'm just so glad to see you back.' The woman patted her on the arm. 'We've really missed you,' she said before hurrying away towards the kitchen.

'And you want to go to a hotel.'

The wry voice from the lounge made Beth turn in surprise. Jay was home. He was standing by the French doors through from the garden.

'You can't leave now,' he said softly. 'She's on a mission to fatten you up. And you know how May likes a challenge.'

'I don't particularly want her to rise to that challenge, though,' she said lightly.

As always the sight of him made her heart speed up, made her feel delighted and at the same time apprehensive.

'This is the second time today you've caught me unawares,' she said. 'I didn't think you would be home so early.'

'Well, we've got unfinished business to discuss, haven't we.' He shrugged nonchalantly, but there was nothing nonchalant about the way his eyes slipped over her.

After she'd unpacked, she'd changed into a pale lilac sundress. It was casual, but it emphasised her slender figure and the wide pansy-blue of her eyes.

'You look lovely, by the way,' he said softly.

'Thanks.' Her heart felt as if it had suddenly moved to her mouth. She walked through to the lounge, conscious of the fact that Jay was watching her every move. She wanted to look attractive, wanted Jay to look at her and regret letting her go, but at the same time she didn't want to appear as if she was trying to impress him. The dress, she had hoped, struck the right balance. Now she wasn't so sure, now she felt acutely self-conscious.

'May hasn't changed a bit,' she said, desperately searching for light conversation.

'No, I don't suppose she has. I don't know what I'd do without her; she's a godsend.'

She stood next to him, the topic of conversation seemingly exhausted as she searched her befuddled brain for something else to say. She noticed that he had changed into a blue shirt and matching chinos, that his hair was slightly damp from a recent shower.

'How long have you been home?'

'About half an hour.'

'You never used to finish work so early.'

'I did sometimes.'

The husky tone of his voice made her heart do a small tap-dance against her ribcage. She wished she could pull her scattered senses together. Wished that she didn't find him so disarmingly attractive.

She pulled her eyes away from the hard, chiselled bone structure, the sensual curve of his lips.

'Would you like a pre-dinner drink?' he offered, moving away from her to open the drinks cabinet. 'You used to like rum and Coke with plenty of ice, as I recall.'

'You've got a good memory.'

He held up the glass and looked at her enquiringly.

'I'll just have a Coke, if you don't mind?'

'No, of course not. We're so polite, aren't we?' he reflected as he poured the drinks. 'No one would ever guess that, when you left here over a year ago, we could barely be civil to each other.'

She looked away from him, uncomfortable with the subject. 'I have to say, it feels strange being back.'

He returned to her side and handed her the drink. Their

fingers brushed momentarily on the frosty glass, yet the heat that shot through Beth was intense.

'Thanks.' She took a deep gulp of the drink, and then coughed as it caught her breath. 'Sorry...' She tried not to cough again and the effort made her eyes water.

'Are you okay?' Jay reached across and patted her on the back. Her dress was cut low with delicate spaghetti straps at the back. The touch of his hand against her naked skin made her catch her breath even more.

'Yes, I'm fine,' she croaked weakly, taking another hasty sip to try and soothe her throat.

His hand rubbed over her back for a moment, his fingers softly caressing against the silky smooth skin. The flare of desire that shot through her caught her completely off balance. 'Really, Jay. I'm fine.' Her voice was sharper than she intended.

'There's no need to bite my head off,' he murmured wryly, stepping away from her.

'I'm sorry.' She cringed. 'To be honest, I'm finding this a bit of a strain.'

'Are you?' He sounded indifferent to her remark. 'Why's that?'

She frowned. 'I would have thought that was obvious. We are separated, yet here we are trying to act as if there is nothing wrong between us, as if we've never been apart. It's bizarre.'

He shrugged. 'A lot of couples separate and remain good friends.'

'Do they?' Elizabeth frowned, trying to think of some.

'We were friends before we got married, why not now?' His dark eyes held hers. Despite the words there was something very sensual about the way he was looking at her. It reminded her of the night of her party. The night they had made love. Was she imagining the chemistry between them?

'So it doesn't bother you?'

'What?'

'Having me here?'

'You've always bothered me.' He grinned. 'Guess I'm used to it.'

When he smiled at her like that she wanted to melt. She was so vulnerable where he was concerned. Why was that? She finished her drink and put the glass down.

'The sun is setting,' Jay remarked idly.

She followed his glance out of the patio doors. The sun was sinking fast, a fierce red flame of colour against a flamingo-pink sea. It was breathtakingly beautiful and for a while it held her attention.

'Shall we go and sit down?' Jay opened the doors through to outside. 'May has set the table out on the patio.'

Beth didn't immediately follow him. 'What's the matter?' He looked around at her enquiringly. 'You used to like eating outside.'

'Yes.' But she'd liked eating alfresco because she had found it romantic. Now she wanted to steer very clear of any hint of romance. 'But I'm suffering from hay fever these days.'

'Really?' He looked concerned and she felt the biggest fraud. 'Well, if you start to sneeze we'll adjourn inside. What do you say?'

He sounded so reasonable that she found herself nodding in compliance.

She followed him around to the end of the terrace, the side that looked down towards the beach. The table was laid with the best silver on a white damask cloth. A small arrangement of flowers holding two white candles flickered invitingly.

He held the chair for her as she sat down.

'I'd forgotten how quickly it goes dark out here,' she

said, looking out to sea as the sun disappeared and a blanket of darkness crept over the landscape.

Jay picked up a bottle that was chilling in an ice bucket beside the table.

'Is that champagne?' Elizabeth asked, her eyebrows lifting.

'Yes…May got it out. She's insisted it would go with her special meal.'

The bottle opened with an explosive pop and he poured the frothy liquid into the champagne flutes with expert ease.

'There.' He handed her a glass and then sat down opposite to her. 'What shall we drink to?'

She hesitated, her eyes holding with his for a second too long. 'How about Cheryl's wedding?'

'Cheryl's wedding it is.' He lifted the glass and touched it against hers. 'May she find happiness and love to last for ever.'

She sipped the drink slowly. She needed to keep a clear head. She wouldn't drink anything more after this, she told herself firmly.

'Almost like old times, isn't it?' Jay remarked.

She met his gaze again, and remembered how he had teased her back in London about the good old days. Suddenly she felt out of her depth. 'Not quite.'

Silence stretched for a moment. 'So how were things at the yard today?' she asked tentatively.

He laughed.

'What? What did I say?'

'Nothing.' His shook his head and his eyes gleamed with humour. 'It's just that you sounded so prim and proper, as if you've decided to be polite and that's the expected question. ''How were things at the office today, dear?'''

Despite herself, Beth grinned. 'Sorry. But I was interested.'

'Well, seeing as you asked, things were pretty hectic. The order I was waiting for arrived, but it wasn't right so I had to send it back, which means we are short of some materials that we desperately need. They say they'll redeliver tomorrow. But whether they do or not is a different matter.'

'Sounds stressful,' she remarked.

'Not really, just the usual kind of day. Luckily I've got a very good team of workers around me, so that helps.'

Did he include Lisa in on that? she wondered. Or did he think in more personal terms when he thought of his secretary? Was he still sleeping with her?

'Sex is just incredible.'

The woman's words played through her mind. She wished she could forget them. She shouldn't care now.

She took another sip of her champagne and tried to turn her mind to more practical things. 'I'll come in with you to the yard tomorrow, if you don't mind?'

'No, of course not.'

'And then I should find another hotel.'

A breeze flickered the candlelight between them and it was hard to read the expression in his eyes as he looked at her.

'What's the point of that? You're here now; you may as well stay.'

'The point is that my being here doesn't feel right.'

'It feels right to me,' he said softly.

'Does it?' Her eyes were uncertain. She felt as if she was treading on very dangerous ground.

If someone had told her a few days ago that she would be staying at Sugar Cane Cottage again, she wouldn't have believed them. She felt as if she had entered into some strange twilight zone where nothing was as it seemed.

'It's nice having you home again, even if it is for a short time,' he said nonchalantly.

Her eyes clashed with his across the table. He was just being polite, she told herself, because for once he needed her.

'What about…your girlfriend. Won't she mind that I'm staying here?' She couldn't bring herself to say Lisa's name; it seemed to stick in her throat.

'Which girlfriend are we talking about?' He grinned.

'You mean there's more than one?'

He smiled. 'Despite everything, you are still my wife. The fact that you're staying here is no one's business but our own.'

Sounded as if Lisa hadn't managed to pin him down. The thought gave her a great deal of pleasure. It made her spirits lift considerably. But it was crazy, really. Probably all it meant was that Jay was his own person and did exactly what he wanted no matter who objected or what the circumstances.

But if Lisa was still on the scene romantically, she couldn't be happy at this situation. Maybe she should stay on for a while just to annoy her. Let the woman have just a tiny taste of her own medicine. The thought made a smile curve her lips.

May came hurrying out with their meals.

'Lobster thermidor,' she said to Elizabeth. 'Especially for you.'

'My favourite!' Elizabeth was overwhelmed at the thoughtful gesture. 'Thank you, May. I'm being well and truly spoilt.'

'No more than you deserve,' May said briskly as she hurried back to the kitchen.

'She's very kind,' Elizabeth said as they were left alone again.

'Well, you do realise that May is one of your greatest fans,' Jay said. 'She gave me hell after you left.'

'I can't imagine anyone giving you hell.' Elizabeth grinned.

'Yeah, well, May did,' he said dryly. 'Kept telling me that I shouldn't have let such a wonderful woman get away.'

'Really?' Elizabeth's eyes gleamed with amusement. 'And what did you say?'

'That I hadn't much choice in the matter. That you were unhappy.'

The amusement died in her eyes.

'I am sorry,' he said quietly.

'Sorry about what?'

'Making you unhappy. It was the last thing I wanted.'

She looked across at him and felt totally bereft for a moment. She did believe that he hadn't set out to hurt her. But somehow it didn't make things better; it just made the pain inside her worse.

They should never have got married. It had been a wild, crazy idea, destined to backfire from the moment she'd suggested it.

She shook her head. 'Let's not talk about the past, Jay. Let's just go forward from here.'

'Okay, but there are things we need to discuss.'

She nodded. 'Yes…the business. Did you manage to reschedule the meetings with the bank?'

He hesitated. 'We have one tomorrow afternoon and another on Thursday morning.'

'That's good. It'll give me a chance to acquaint myself with the accounts and the state of the business in the morning.'

She noted an enigmatic smile curving the strong line of his lips. What was he thinking? she wondered. For a moment she felt there was something else going on here, some hidden agenda. Then she dismissed the notion. What else could be going on? As always, he was just thinking about the business.

'And if you don't mind I'll have to ring my office in London tomorrow morning as well.'

'Why's that?' Jay asked.

'I promised John I'd leave a number where I could be contacted.'

'Such devotion and dedication to work,' Jay reflected drolly.

'I was in the middle of a big account.' Elizabeth shrugged. 'Colin's taken over, but if there are any teething problems they need to be able to reach me.'

'And I suppose John doesn't like you too far out of his sights?'

'I wouldn't go so far as to say that,' Elizabeth said, frowning. 'No one is indispensable.'

'So leave them to muddle through, then.'

'I can't do that.' She looked at him, horrified.

'There is such a thing as being too conscientious, Beth. And sometimes you're no better thought of for it.'

'John thinks very highly of me,' she said.

'But will he leave his wife for you?' Jay asked quietly.

'I beg your pardon?' She stared at him, bewildered.

'It's John, isn't it? This guy you are seeing?'

She felt her face go bright pink with embarrassment. He thought she was having an affair with John! She wanted to say, There is no guy, but that would only make her look incredibly foolish now. 'That's absurd,' she spluttered. 'No, it isn't John. He's my boss and, as you so rightly pointed out, he's married.'

Jay watched her, watched the way her face suffused with colour, the strained note in her voice. She was lying; it was John; he was sure of it now.

'Yes, he's married, and married men tend to like the

best of both worlds,' Jay continued briskly. 'They like the security of having a wife and the excitement of having a mistress.'

'Speaking from experience, are you, Jay?' she snapped.

'I'm speaking as someone who cares about you and doesn't want to see you get hurt,' Jay said gently.

'Well, then, mind your own business.'

He shrugged. 'Maybe I shouldn't have said anything, but—'

'I am not having an affair with John,' she cut across him fiercely.

They both fell silent as the door through from the kitchen opened and May came out to clear away the dishes.

'That was delicious, May,' Elizabeth said, glad of the diversion.

'I'm glad you liked it. I'll leave you to finish your drinks.' The woman nodded. 'I'll serve coffee and pudding in the lounge, if you'd like?'

'Thanks, May.'

There was silence after she left them.

Elizabeth's eyes still glimmered with fury as they met Jay's across the table.

'Look, I'm sorry. Shall we just leave it at that?' he said impatiently.

'You have no right to question me about my private life.' She shook her head, unable to leave the subject.

'I am still your husband,' he said quietly.

'Theoretically. But it's just words on a piece of paper.'

'I suppose it is.' He met her eyes levelly. 'Although I think some people might take exception to such a cynical view of marriage.'

'I wasn't talking about marriage in general. I was talking about our marriage.'

'Never an easy subject at the best of times,' he agreed wryly.

'No.'

She finished her glass of champagne.

'I just had your best interests at heart,' he said gently. 'But you're quite right: who you choose to see is your affair.'

She didn't like his choice of words.

Below them she could see the white surf as it rolled against the beach. She remembered their wedding night. They had dined out here, alone on the terrace.

Even then she had felt tension between them. The old easiness with which they had used to laugh at nothing had gone, and had been replaced by the seriousness and the enormity of what they had done.

After dinner they had walked along the shore, Jay had reached for her hand and pulled her close. Then he had kissed her. It had been a kiss unlike any other; it had set her on fire... It had kindled something inside her that had never seemed to die, no matter what had happened between them.

'What are you thinking about?' Jay's voice pulled her thoughts away from the abyss of that memory.

She glanced over at him. 'Nothing much.' She couldn't tell him she'd been thinking about their wedding night. She shouldn't be thinking about things like that. It was only stirring up the past, making the present so much more difficult.

'Would you like to have a stroll along the beach before we have coffee?' Jay asked suddenly.

She felt herself tense. He had probably forgotten all about their first night together, she told herself fiercely. Otherwise he never would have suggested such a thing.

But how could he forget the wild passion of that first time? The way they had undressed each other under the stars, their kisses fervent, intense. Even now, her skin felt as if it was tingling as she remembered the way they had lain down together on that deserted beach, the warm tide flooding around them, sweet against the sensitised heat of their naked bodies.

She couldn't meet the darkness of his gaze. 'No, thanks, Jay. In fact I'm going to turn in, if you don't mind. I'm a bit tired.'

'Don't you want coffee, or dessert?'

She shook her head.

'It's no wonder you are looking so thin.'

'I'm not thin.'

'You've lost a lot of your curves.' He took a sip of his champagne and regarded her steadily across the table. 'Curves that I always rather liked.'

She avoided looking at him, uncomfortable with the subject. He hadn't liked her curves at all. She remembered Lisa making a derisive comment about her figure... But of course Lisa could afford to mock: she was stick-thin. And Jay had chosen her to have an affair with her. 'I was overweight.'

'You were never overweight.' Jay sounded horrified. 'You had a very desirable figure. If anything, you are too thin now.'

'I'm happy being a size smaller,' she said firmly.

Jay shook his head. 'You know it's a fallacy that men prefer skinny women, don't you?'

'And do you know it's a fallacy that women want to be thin to please men? We really don't give a damn what men think of us at all.'

'Good job, because I reckon any man would tell you to eat your chocolate cake,' he said with a grin.

'Not every man.' She was stung to retort.

'Really?' Jay's voice was dry. 'Is that why you've lost weight? To please your boyfriend?'

'No. I told you. I've pleased myself.' Actually she hadn't tried to lose weight at all; it had dropped off her when she had left Jay. 'And I've only gone down one dress size. I'm not that thin!'

'I think you are.' He grinned at her. 'Plus you've lost curves from strategic places... I noticed when we spent the night together in London—'

'Jay, stop it.' Her heart hammered fiercely against her chest now. 'I don't want to talk about what happened between us in London.'

'There's not a lot left that we can talk about...is there?' he said dryly.

She pushed her chair back from the table. 'There's the boat yard. It's why I'm here. Remember?'

'Of course I remember.' He finished his champagne. 'But before we move towards business...I would like to know if there were any repercussions from our night together.'

The nonchalant question made her nerves stretch tightly.

She didn't answer him for a moment.

He held her gaze.

What would he say if she was pregnant? she wondered. What would he suggest they do? Get a termination? The idea made her feel ill.

'If there's anything to tell...I'll tell you,' she said calmly, getting up from the table. 'Now, if you'll excuse me...'

CHAPTER EIGHT

ELIZABETH woke up at five-thirty in the morning and lay staring up into the darkness of her room, wondering why she was so wide awake, until she realised that it was ten-thirty in the morning in London.

She tried to think about the office, wondered how Colin was going on with her account. But her mind kept veering back towards Jay and their conversation last night.

She swung her legs out of bed and put her dressing gown on. There was no way she was going to get back to sleep now, she thought angrily. Might as well go downstairs and get a drink.

It was still dark outside; the first pearly morning light was just a faint spark on the horizon. She poured herself a glass of water from a bottle in the fridge, and then brought it through to the lounge to sit in one of the comfortable settees and watch the dawn break.

That was where Jay found her over an hour later, curled up against the cushions fast asleep. The blue silk dressing gown had fallen open, revealing the lacy nightdress beneath and a provocative glimpse of satin-soft skin.

He allowed himself to watch her for a few moments. And remembered when she had shared the huge double bed in the other room with him. Remembered watching her sometimes after they had made love, when exhaustion had claimed her and she'd lain vulnerable and warm in his arms. The memory stirred desire instantly to life.

He wanted her back in his bed. Wanted to hold her and make love to her again.

Her eyes flickered open, wide and blue and misted by sleep.

'Good morning.' He smiled at her. 'Wasn't your bed comfortable? Or do you prefer sleeping on the settee these days?'

'Sorry!' She looked around her, as if amazed to find herself in the living room. 'I don't know what happened; one moment I was wide awake, the next, out of it totally.' She sat up, pulling her dressing gown firmly around her figure, running a self-conscious hand through her short hair.

He was fully dressed, she noticed, wearing jeans and a T-shirt. 'What time is it?'

'Almost seven. Would you like some breakfast? I was about to make myself some coffee and toast, but I can run to bacon and eggs if you'd prefer.'

She shook her head. 'Just coffee would be fine.' She stood up. 'I'll go and get dressed.'

'Don't bother on my account.' He grinned. 'I've seen you in far less.'

The husky tones made her blush, but they also stirred something deeper than embarrassment. They stirred a feeling of latent desire, a feeling that fired her body with a need so fierce that it dazed her.

'There is just the two of us in the house. May is down at her son's place, and probably won't be back until lunch-time.'

Jay moved away from her towards the kitchen.

She was glad he was moving away from her, glad she had a chance to gather herself together. She was still half asleep, that was what was wrong with her, she told herself. She didn't really have any desire for Jay. Not any more.

'How did you sleep?'

'Apart from waking so early, fine,' she said vaguely.

He smiled. 'You haven't woken up yet, have you?'

Making sure that her dressing gown was securely fastened, she followed him to the door. 'No...not quite,' she admitted ruefully.

'Come on, I'll get you that coffee.'

She followed him into the kitchen and he pulled out one of the stools at the breakfast bar for her to sit down.

She watched him as he moved efficiently around the modern kitchen, grinding some coffee beans, getting out some china beakers. The smell of the coffee drifted on the warm morning air, suddenly making her feel hungry.

'How about some croissants?' He flicked a look of enquiry over at her, as if he had read her mind.

'That would be nice, thanks.'

Outside the windows she could see a perfect blue sky through the tracery of the palm trees. It was another hot, wonderful day. Hard to believe that back in London people would be wearing thick coats and hats to keep out the February chill.

It was good to be back here. Good to be sitting in her kitchen again. Everything felt so normal, she thought. As if she had never been away.

He put the coffee and croissants down beside her.

'It looks really hot out there,' Elizabeth remarked turning her attention from the garden.

'Coolest time of the day.' He smiled. 'If you want to have a dip in the pool before we leave for the yard, now is a good time.'

'No...maybe later.'

She sipped the coffee; it tasted good, better than anything she had tasted in a long time.

'We didn't seem to get off to a very good start over dinner last night, did we?' Jay remarked suddenly. 'I shouldn't have asked about John...maybe it was insensitive of me.'

Jay watched her, noted the faint blush on her high

cheekbones, the softness of her lips, the dark thick sweep of her eyelashes that seemed to hide her away from him so well.

She shrugged. 'I was a bit tired last night…perhaps a bit touchy…we'll forget about it, shall we?'

'Fine. So are we friends again?'

The dark eyes that held hers sent a tremor of awareness through her. 'Yes, friends.' She smiled lightly.

He reached across and for one heart-stopping moment she thought he was going to kiss her. But his lips just brushed lightly against her cheek.

'Good.' He pulled back. 'I'm glad. It makes everything so much easier.'

'For the yard?' She sought clarification, even though she knew that was what he meant.

'Yes…of course.'

The phone in the hall started to ring. Jay let it go on for a while before reluctantly standing up. 'I suppose I had better see who that is.'

Elizabeth pressed her fingers against her lips trying to stem the tingling sensation that threatened to engulf her. She'd wanted him to kiss her. The need had been quite frightening, the disappointment intense.

What was the matter with her? she wondered angrily. Sometimes she didn't think she understood herself at all.

She took a sip of her coffee, trying to put the episode out of her mind.

'That was the suppliers assuring me they will be delivering today,' Jay said briskly as he returned. 'Although, seeing is believing.'

'It was good of them to ring,' she said. 'Sounds like they'll follow through.'

'Maybe.' He finished his coffee. 'I'd better get going. Are you coming with me, or do you want to drive yourself in later? Your car is still in the garage.'

'No. I'll come with you.'

'Okay, but I'll have to leave in about twenty minutes.'

'I'll be ten,' she assured him, hurriedly finishing her drink.

She didn't have time to agonise over what she should wear, so she just flung on the first thing that came to hand: a pink sundress that stopped just above the knee.

It wasn't until they were driving to the yard and she noticed Jay glancing at her legs that she wondered if she should have worn something that covered her up more. Although she had sat in the sun yesterday when she'd been waiting for Jay, her legs were still slightly white.

'You're right, I'll have to sit in the sun before I go back to London,' she said cheerfully. 'I look awful in this short dress.'

Jay glanced over at her again. 'I was just thinking how good you look in it,' he said nonchalantly. 'You always did have very shapely legs.'

'I don't think you should be noticing things like that,' she said, trying to ignore the pleasure that flowed through her at the compliment.

He glanced over at her, amusement dancing in his dark eyes. 'Elizabeth, the day I stop noticing things like that is the day they will be lowering me into the ground.'

'Yes, you always were a red-blooded male,' she agreed wryly.

Jay swerved to avoid a pothole in the road and his concentration was firmly on the twists and turns in the road until they pulled through the gates to the boat yard.

The last time Elizabeth had seen the business it had been a small building with a couple of jetties and a slipway which led down into a pretty bay. Her father had probably employed about thirty people. Now she wondered if she was looking at the same place. It was enormous. There were two massive warehouses that housed a staggering amount of boats and labourers. New jetties and a new slip-way made for bigger vessels.

'So, what do you think, partner?' Jay asked jauntily as he parked in the shade.

'It's great.' She shook her head, totally amazed. 'I had no idea you had done so much with the place.'

'Well, you would have done if you'd read the reports I faxed through to you,' he said. 'Didn't you even look at them?'

'Yes, of course I did.'

He looked at her with disbelief. 'If the way you treated the last lot of papers is anything to go by. I suppose they lay on your desk, never to be glanced at.'

'I did look at them.' She remembered the official-looking documents coming through into her office at home. Remembered scanning them as they came out of the machine, hoping for a personal message, a sign that maybe he was missing her, but they had only been concerned with the yard. 'I always look at my faxes. Maybe you should have faxed the last lot of papers instead of sending them by courier.'

'You're full of horse manure sometimes, Elizabeth Hammond.' He looked over at her, his dark eyes gleaming with amusement. 'You didn't read those faxes that closely. There were a few things that needed your signature and you never returned them. Which was precisely why I made you sign for the last lot.'

'Well...maybe I felt I didn't need to read them that closely.' She admitted softly. 'I trusted you.'

'Did you?' His eyes moved over her face searchingly.

'Of course I did. Dad always said you knew what you were doing at the yard. He trusted you implicitly, so why shouldn't I?'

'I'm flattered.' Jay's voice was sardonic. He opened the

Jeep door into the blast of the morning heat. 'Come on, I'll show you around.'

As she followed him past a line of boats in different stages of assembly, her eyes flicked up to where her father's office used to be. Was Lisa in there? she wondered. And all of a sudden she didn't feel at all well.

She didn't know if she could face Lisa. It was one thing trying to put the past behind her, but she didn't think she was ready to face old ghouls from it.

'As you can see I've invested heavily in new technology,' Jay was saying. He raised his voice as the noise of machinery started up. 'It's been necessary to secure the good contracts. I've also quadrupled the amount of staff.'

'I don't recognise any old faces,' she managed to say nonchalantly looking around, pretending a relaxed air that she certainly didn't possess.

'There's one or two,' he said.

The noise levels around them increased. 'Come on up to the office,' Jay was practically shouting now. 'It's quieter up there.'

He turned to lead the way up the wooden steps to the old section of the yard.

She remembered going up here the night she had found Jay and Lisa alone. Remembered seeing them through the glass door.

'You'll find things haven't changed too much up here,' he shouted over his shoulder to her. 'Obviously everything is computerised now, but some things are reassuringly the same.'

She saw the glass door and felt her chest tighten as she anticipated coming face to face with her old rival.

He pushed it open.

'Morning, Jay. You've had two calls from Ben Riding. I told him you'd ring back as soon as you got in,' a female voice said briskly.

Elizabeth looked over at the woman seated behind the desk in the outer office. Young, blonde and attractive...but it wasn't Lisa.

Elizabeth felt as if a weight had been lifted off her shoulders. The relief was immense.

'Thanks, Caroline.' Jay smiled at the woman. 'By the way this is my wife, Elizabeth. Elizabeth, meet Caroline, my secretary.'

Caroline gave her a brief smile as she reached to pick up some files.

Elizabeth smiled back. But she was thinking about the buzz she felt at being introduced as Jay's wife. It felt good. It was a crazy reaction... What was in a title, after all...? Nothing. They were just words.

Jay ushered her swiftly through the door leading into his private office.

She noticed that Jay still had her father's desk and chair, and his photograph still sat where she had placed it many years ago. But apart from that the inner sanctum was different. It was bigger; there were sloping design tables at one side and several computers. And the walls at one side were glass. Looking down over the yard from this vantage point was vastly different from what it had been in her father's day.

'So, what do you think?' Jay asked.

'I think it's great.'

Jay grinned. 'It will be when we get the go ahead from the bank to do another extension.'

'Do we need another? You've done so much.'

'We still need to expand further. I'm turning down orders at the moment because we're not big enough to deal with them.'

There was a tap on the door and Caroline put her head around. 'Jay, that order you were expecting is here. Do you want to come and check it?'

'I'll be right there.' Jay looked over at Beth. 'I won't be long. Sit down and pour yourself a coffee.' He indicated the coffee machine by the windows.

As the door closed behind him, Beth looked around the office. It felt really weird being back here. She could almost imagine that her dad might walk into the room at any moment. Nice to see you, sweetheart, he would say, with that usual cheery smile.

God, she missed him. Her hand trailed over the smooth wood of his desk, the desk he had sat behind for many years. Her eyes moved to his photograph.

'The will was a bad mistake,' she told him gently. 'I know you were trying to help, I know you thought Jay was right for me…but it was a mad idea.'

She'd always been close to her father. His death had been a terrible shock. Cheryl had been devastated as well. Elizabeth was looking forward to seeing her again. She'd always got on well with her stepmother. It was sad that they had lost touch with each other since her father's death. She supposed that, like her, Cheryl had been struggling to come to terms with everything.

Elizabeth poured herself a coffee and stood looking out of the windows down at the technologically advanced yard. She had to hand it to Jay, he'd thoroughly transformed the place.

The door opened behind her and, thinking it was Jay, she turned with a smile.

It wasn't Jay, it was Lisa.

For a moment she didn't know who looked more surprised, her, or the woman standing framed in the doorway.

Elizabeth was the first to pull herself together. 'Hello, Lisa,' she said coolly.

'Hi.' The woman didn't smile at Elizabeth. She was as beautiful as ever, Elizabeth noted. Her long blonde hair was swept back from her face in a classical chignon, revealing a perfectly shaped face with wide golden brown eyes.

She wandered over towards the desk and put a file down. She was wearing a grey pencil skirt and a short-sleeved white blouse that dipped provocatively low at the neckline.

'Jay didn't tell me you were coming in today,' she said.

'Was he supposed to?' Elizabeth asked coolly.

Lisa smiled and changed the subject. 'What do you think of the yard? Great, isn't it?'

'Jay has worked very hard,' Elizabeth agreed.

'Yes…he's been tearing his hair out, poor guy. I told him to go and see you in London. You never achieve anything with faxes and phone calls.'

'Well, nothing of a personal nature anyway,' Elizabeth agreed smoothly, and was somewhat mollified to see the flare of annoyance in the other woman's eyes.

'How do you like life in London?' Lisa asked suddenly. 'Jay was telling me that things are working out for you very well.'

'Yes, they are.' What else had Jay been telling her? she wondered. It really rankled to think of Jay discussing her with this woman. Perhaps it was time to clarify a few points. 'But it's good being back home,' she said sweetly. 'Sugar Cane Cottage is such a lovely place. Jay and I had dinner last night out on the patio, and it was as if I'd never been away.'

Elizabeth had never been a bitchy person, but she had to admit it was gratifying to be able to turn the tables on Lisa. Let her wonder what was going on, let invidious jealousy keep her awake at night… serve her damn well right!

'Well, I'm pleased,' Lisa said, although she looked anything but. 'Jay has been waiting a long time to sort things out with the business. And it's good you are both being so civilised about things.'

'Oh, we're being more than civilised,' Elizabeth assured her.

'Well, nice talking to you Elizabeth.' The woman smiled. 'Hope to see you again, before you go.'

Then she turned and left the room, her hips swaying from side to side in the tight grey pencil skirt.

She had to have the last word, didn't she? Elizabeth thought with annoyance.

What was the state of play with Lisa and Jay? she wondered. And why had Jay got a new secretary? Surely he didn't need two private secretaries? She finished her coffee and tried to tell herself that she didn't care what was going on in Jay's personal life.

A few minutes later, Jay swept back into the room. 'Did Lisa bring the accounts over?' His eyes lighted on the file. 'Ah, I see she did. Great. They are for you to peruse.'

'Why have you got two secretaries these days?' Elizabeth asked dryly. 'Wasn't one enough for you?'

Jay was flicking through the file. 'Lisa is working in the accounts office now, on the other side of the yard.'

'Why have you moved her to Accounts?' She waited for him to tell her they were dating, or an item. She supposed under those circumstances it was best to work apart, otherwise his supremacy as boss might clash with his role as lover.

'I just thought she was best suited to the job over there,' he replied nonchalantly. He passed the file over to her. 'Do you want to sit in here to go through these? Or would you rather go home and read them?'

'No, I'll stay here.' She pulled out the chair from behind his desk, and tried to focus only on business. 'Have you got the order book as well, or is all that computerised now?'

'It is, but I've kept the book updated as well...just in case the systems go down.' He opened up a drawer and handed it to her with a grin. 'Some habits die hard even with all this modern technology.'

She smiled coolly and took the book. She didn't feel like responding to that warm charm of his right now. In fact she wanted to tell him to go to hell.

Not only had he promoted his lover, but he was also still pretending that there was nothing personal between them. It was totally sickening.

Her eyes flicked over the lists of figures.

'Would you like another coffee?' Jay asked.

'Yes, thanks.' She didn't look up. 'There's quite a lot to get through here. What time are we meeting your bank manager?'

'Three o'clock, but I'll have to ring him and change it.'

'Why?' She looked up at him as he placed the mug of coffee beside her.

'Because we'd arranged to meet at the golf club, discuss business over a round of golf. When I made the arrangement I didn't realise you'd be here. But it's no problem; we'll just change the venue. George is usually flexible'

'Don't bother on my account. I'll play a round with you.'

'Now, that's the best offer I've had in ages,' Jay remarked with a grin.

'You know what I mean, Jay. A round of golf.' She glanced up at him, her blue eyes piercingly intent.

He shrugged, the humour still apparent in his eyes. 'Pity.'

She looked back at the figures in front of her. The man had a damn nerve trying to flirt with her.

'I didn't know you could play golf,' Jay said, perching on the edge of the desk.

'I learnt when I was in London,' she murmured, trying

to concentrate on the accounts and not on how close he was to her. 'I found that most of the men in the office were conducting business that way…so I decided to join the club.'

'Good for you.'

Elizabeth frowned, wondering if he was being patronising now.

'But I think we should leave the golf for another time,' he continued. 'We don't want to be out on the course for too long in the heat of the day.'

'In other words, you think I won't be able to play very well and I'll slow things down?'

'No, of course not.'

Her eyes moved over the handsome features in disbelief. 'Yes, you do, admit it.'

'Not at all. I was just thinking about you. It will still be pretty hot at three o'clock, and you haven't given yourself much chance to acclimatise to it yet. Plus you must still be a bit tired from all your travelling.'

'You're so considerate, Jay,' she drawled sarcastically. 'But I'm not tired, and I'll cope with the heat.'

'Okay.' He shrugged and got off the desk. 'What's your handicap, by the way?' he asked nonchalantly.

Her lips curved. He really thought she wouldn't be able to play. He was so chauvinistic sometimes. 'Handicap?' She looked up at him blankly. 'Goes by the name of Jay Hammond, I think.'

He smiled and shook his head. 'We better stop off at home on the way to the club. Get you some sun cream and a hat.'

'Good idea; it will give me an opportunity to change.' She returned her attention to the accounts. 'Oh, and can I use the phone here to call my office? I need to give them those contact numbers.'

Jay shrugged. 'If you want.'

*   *   *

The club hit the ball with a firm whack; then they watched as it flew smoothly down the fairway to land exactly a few feet away from the hole.

'You're supposed to be playing golf with our bank manager, Beth, not slaughtering the guy,' Jay murmured in an undertone.

'I'm sorry! You mean, I've got to allow the man to win, otherwise we might not get our bank loan?' She batted wide eyes up at him in mock innocence.

He grinned. 'Something like that,' he agreed dryly.

'Perfect shot, Elizabeth.' George Brewer caught up with them. 'You're a very accomplished player.'

'Thank you, George.' She smiled at him. He was about twenty-eight, and a very handsome man.

They watched while Jay positioned himself to play his shot.

'So, Elizabeth, have you given any further thought to the idea of Jay buying you out of the business?' George asked nonchalantly.

'No…to be honest, I haven't,' Elizabeth said firmly. 'The business was set up by my father and that's a very strong tie for me. But I am happy to let Jay have the driving seat. He's done a wonderful job with it so far. I think it's just going to go from strength to strength now.'

'Yes, it certainly is very healthy at the moment. But don't you think that having a business partner so far away is a hindrance to the company's development?'

'No.' Elizabeth was firm. 'In this era of modern technology, no one is more than the push of a button away. Jay and I are in constant contact. We fax each other regularly, and we work in complete harmony. I think it's an arrangement that works very well.'

Jay hit the ball slightly off balance and it landed well short of where it was supposed to go.

'Looks like you are thrashing us both now,' George observed with a laugh.

'It does, doesn't it?' Elizabeth grinned at Jay as he turned to look at her.

They walked to the eighteenth green. The sun was blistering down out of a clear blue sky. Elizabeth was glad the game was nearing completion. Although she was in the lead, it had been a toughly fought battle. And what with the constant questions about the business from their bank manager, and the heat, she was ready to call it a day.

She played and the ball slipped down sweetly in one.

'Well done.' George grinned as he stepped forward to play.

'Hard luck,' Elizabeth murmured to Jay as he came to stand next to her.

'I was distracted.' He grinned. His gaze moved over her shapely figure in the white shorts and T-shirt. For a second she thought he was flirting with her, and then he grinned. 'I had to listen to you talking a load of rubbish; it would have put anyone off their game.'

She shook her head, a glimmer of humour in her blue eyes. 'No one likes a sore loser, Jay,' she admonished lightly.

He laughed, unperturbed. 'But you were spouting a lot of rubbish.' Rich amusement laced the deep timber of his voice. 'Remind me now, when was the last time you sent me a fax?'

She shrugged airily, a small smile curving the softness of her lips. 'You told me I had to impress upon him how united we were, how well our partnership worked. You said if I didn't we might not get our bank loan. I was only doing as I was told.'

'The day you do as you're told, I'll have to have heart surgery to heal the shock.'

'Didn't think you had a heart,' she replied wryly.

'Didn't you?' He looked down at her. 'Maybe I can prove that to you later.'

The gentleness of his tone and the way he looked at her broke the teasing banter. She glanced away from him, confused suddenly. Was he just so used to flirting with women that he did it automatically? she wondered. Or was this all part of the game to win her over, make her sell her shares in the company to him?

'Shall we adjourn to the clubhouse and have a drink?' Jay asked as George came back over to join them.

'I'd love to, but I'm going to have to get off. I've got business back at the bank before I can go home.'

Jay nodded. 'Okay. We'll see you on Thursday, then, George. We can talk things over in more detail then.'

'Yes, meanwhile I'll study your application again. Talk over your request with the area manager.' George murmured easily. 'As you know, we were a bit concerned with Elizabeth's absence. But today has clarified a few things.'

As they walked back to the clubhouse, Jay slipped an arm around her waist. It was just a nonchalant gesture, but it made Elizabeth profoundly conscious of his closeness, of the fact that his merest touch made her tremble inside with a longing she didn't want to acknowledge.

She would have pulled away from him, only she didn't want to create a scene in front of George.

The man shook hands with them both by the front steps to the club. 'Nice to have met you finally, Elizabeth,' he said pleasantly. 'I'll look forward to seeing you Thursday morning.'

As he turned to walk away towards his shiny red Porsche, Jay let his hand slip away from her.

'He was very keen for me to sell my half of the business out to you, wasn't he?' Elizabeth murmured. 'I must have told him three times I wasn't interested.'

'I told you. The bank wants to simplify matters. And maybe he's testing your commitment.'

'My commitment to the business is very strong. I couldn't have made that clearer.'

'Couldn't you?' Jay shrugged. 'I think the bank looks on the matter in a slightly more clinical light. Your commitment to me is broken, therefore there's a question mark over your role in the future of the business.'

'You still think I should sell to you, don't you?'

'Yes, part of me thinks it would be for the best,' he admitted softly. 'But I'm impatient to proceed with expanding the business. So, for the time being, I'll settle for them okaying my application for a loan.' He turned away from her. 'Come on, I'll buy you a drink,' he said, changing the subject.

Should she sell to Jay and just call it quits? she wondered as she sat in the elegant lounge of the clubhouse? What would her father have thought if he were here now?

It was starting to go dark outside. Elizabeth sat nursing a glass of mineral water and watched the sun slowly sinking over the well-manicured gardens of the club. The chair was very comfortable and so was the bliss of the air-conditioning.

Jay had been right about the fact she hadn't acclimatised yet to the temperatures. The heat had really got to her this afternoon out on the golf course. She felt drained from it and a little bit nauseous. It was strange, because it had never used to bother her when she'd lived here. Maybe it was just jet lag.

'What did you think of George?' Jay asked casually as he sipped his glass of beer.

'I thought he was a very pleasant guy. But very young to be a bank manager.' She grinned. 'Do you think that's a sign of old age...you know, like when you think policemen are looking younger by the day?'

Jay laughed. 'Well, if it is, we're growing old together. I thought the very same thing when I first met him.'

Growing old together was one thing they would never do, she thought matter-of-factly. The thought made her feel unaccountably sad. She pulled herself up sharply. She had a life in London to get back to. A life she loved. And one day she'd meet someone else, someone who truly loved her.

The words rang hollowly inside her. She didn't want to meet anyone else. She glanced across at Jay. She wanted him. She still loved him.

The realisation hit her out of nowhere like a body blow.

'Would you like to stay and have some dinner here?' Jay asked. 'I can ring May and tell her to have the evening off.'

'No…I'd like to get back, if you don't mind. Shower and change.' She sounded brisk, no hint of the emotion inside. 'And also I must make some enquiries about a hotel.'

'I thought you'd decided to stay on at the house for a while longer?'

'No…really, I can't.' She looked away from him.

'Why not?'

'Because…it's too awkward.'

'Is it?' Jay shrugged. 'Or is it because your boyfriend has objected to your choice of lodgings?'

'Nobody has objected to anything,' she said swiftly.

Despite the vehement protest, Jay didn't believe her. This morning, when they had sat having breakfast together, he could have sworn that the mood between them had been good. She had seemed happy, relaxed. Since coming into the office and ringing London her mood had changed.

Once more that wary, almost hostile, light was in her eyes. It reminded him of the last weeks of their marriage, when she had withdrawn totally into herself. He hadn't been able to reach her at all, not with humour, or gentle teasing…or lovemaking. Nothing had worked, and when he had pressed her too far she had just snapped.

In the aftermath of her leaving he had sometimes wondered if he had let her go too easily, if he should have fought to make her stay.

But she had obviously not been thinking straight when she had suggested they marry. She had been stricken with grief over her father. It stood to sense that given time she might turn around and realise she'd made a mistake.

So he'd let her go. At the back of his mind he had hoped that, by giving her freedom and space to recover, she might come back.

He'd given it a couple of months and then unable to stand it any longer, he'd followed her to London. He had told himself it was primarily a business trip to finalise design details on the British yacht, and that while he was there he'd just casually look her up.

However, when he'd pulled into her road she had been on her way out. He'd watched from further down the street as she'd walked towards a car with a group of friends. She had been laughing and joking and she had looked so radiantly happy it had given him a gut-wrenching feeling inside.

He'd turned around and left. Had told himself that at least she was happy, and that was all he'd been concerned about. And if she wanted him, she knew where he was. Then he'd tried to forget about her…which had been much easier said than done.

He watched her now, and wanted to reach across and shake her. Either that or take her into his arms and kiss her senseless.

He knew she had some feelings for him. Hell, she was so passionate in bed, for one thing…so warm and responsive.

But good sex didn't mean that someone loved you. And maybe this guy in London was able to reach her on a deeper level. Or maybe Elizabeth just needed to be self-sufficient. No ties, no commitment. He half understood that. It was how he'd felt after his divorce.

'Shall we go?' She smiled at him coolly.

'Sure.' He finished his beer. 'Whatever you say.'

She looked at him through narrowed eyes. 'You're not really annoyed that I beat you at golf, are you?' she asked suddenly.

He smiled at that. 'No, of course not.'

'But you didn't think I'd be able to play?'

'Oh, Elizabeth, I never doubted that you could play for one minute,' he drawled. 'The man who underestimated you would be a very foolish one indeed.'

'True…' She frowned, wondering if she was imagining the edge to his voice. 'You weren't thinking about golf just now, were you?'

'Another hole in one.' He smiled.

'What were you thinking about…? The business? Buying my shares?'

'If you must know I was wondering if you needed this guy you're dating in London.'

The question startled her. 'Need him…?' She felt herself growing hot and uncomfortable. 'In what way?'

Jay's lips curved in a sardonic smile. 'Don't look so apprehensive, I wasn't talking about sex. I just wondered if he was someone you liked to have around. Someone to curl up with and watch TV, someone to scrub your back in the bath—'

'You said you weren't talking about sex,' she cut across him warningly.

'All right, do you ring him up and ask him to kill spiders for you, and take the lids off jars?' he grated sardonically. 'In short, do you miss him when he's not around?'

'Kill spiders and take the tops off jars?' Her lips twitched with amusement.

'Well, let me put it another way,' he said, throwing discretion out of the window. 'Do you hope he'll leave his wife and make an honest woman of you?'

She tried to look away from him, but his eyes were deeply probing and somehow filled with a silent challenge. The feeling confused her. 'I am an honest woman,' she said firmly.

He shook his head. 'It doesn't matter. Come on, let's go.'

She didn't argue with him, didn't want to get into the realms of her mythical boyfriend in London. But she wondered why he'd asked her that.

CHAPTER NINE

THEY hardly spoke on the way home. Jay seemed to be annoyed with her for some reason. Would he have liked her to say she was deeply in love with the supposed boyfriend?

She remembered before her father had died, when she had been able to talk with Jay about most things in a frank and easy manner. Sometimes they had shared a beer together after the boat yard had closed on a Saturday. And Jay would ask casually if she had a date for the evening. Sometimes she had…sometimes she hadn't. She'd never lied to him, had always told him the truth, that they were just casual dates…nothing serious.

Was Jay hoping for a return to those days of friendship? Had he wanted her to talk about her relationship as if they were long-lost buddies out having a beer? She bit down on her lip. That was a part she had played once, but could never play again. Especially since they had crossed the line to more intimate times.

But she didn't love him, she told herself fiercely, as she watched the powerful headlights illuminating the dark winding roads. It was just that you couldn't go back. Couldn't be a casual friend to someone when you remembered too vividly how it felt to be a lover.

She glanced across at him. She didn't love him, she told herself firmly again. Her brain was playing tricks on her. It was being back in Jamaica that was unsettling her. Yes, that was what it was, just a bad case of nostalgia.

'Cheryl should be arriving from Florida tomorrow

night,' she said lightly, trying to focus her mind on something else.

'The wedding is on Saturday, isn't it?'

'Yes…Saturday.' Elizabeth nodded.

'Shall we drive out to the airport together and pick her and her partner up?'

'That would be nice,' Elizabeth agreed.

'Where are they staying, do you know?'

Elizabeth paused for a moment before telling him. 'The hotel where we got married.'

'Really?' He glanced across at her.

'She said she thought it was a very romantic location for a wedding.'

'Well, I suppose it was.'

Once more there was silence between them. Elizabeth wished that Cheryl had chosen another location for the wedding. Going back there was the one thing she wasn't looking forward to. It would be like facing the past…the scene of the crime revisited. She smiled to herself. Idiot, she mocked herself lightly.

When they pulled to a halt in front of Jay's house, the front door opened and May came hurrying outside to meet them on the drive.

'Jay, I've got to go over to my son's house,' she said anxiously. 'My daughter-in-law has fallen down some steps. Jake has taken her into hospital, but they need someone to look after Paul, the baby.'

'I'll take you over there,' Jay offered immediately.

'No, I can drive myself,' the woman said briskly. 'But I have only just started to prepare the evening meal and I didn't want to leave without explaining—'

'Oh, for goodness' sake, May, don't worry about the meal,' Elizabeth said putting a soothing hand on her arm. 'You go to your family. Are you sure you are in a fit state to drive? Do you want me to come with you?'

'No…I'm fine. Thank you, Elizabeth.' The woman hurried away towards her car. 'I'll ring you later,' she called over her shoulder.

'How terrible,' Elizabeth murmured as they went inside. 'I do hope that her daughter-in-law and the baby she is carrying are both going to be all right.'

'Well, they are in the best place,' Jay reassured her, with a worried look on his face.

There was a delicious smell of cooking emanating from the kitchen.

Elizabeth walked through to investigate. 'I can't believe that May was worrying about our meal. She should have just left everything.'

'Yes, but that's May. She's too conscientious sometimes.'

Beth bent down and opened the oven door to look in. 'Loin of pork with a herb and apple stuffing,' she said, closing the door again. 'Shall I put a few roast potatoes and vegetables in there?'

'Not unless you are hungry.' Jay shook his head. 'A side salad will be fine for me.'

'Yes…me too.' She opened the fridge to investigate.

'Like old times, seeing you in here,' Jay remarked suddenly from the doorway behind her.

'As I recall, I never did a lot of cooking.'

'You did a bit. Do you remember the time you incinerated the Beef Wellington?'

She felt her body heat up at the memory. 'No, I don't remember that,' she lied. But she could remember it very clearly. They had only been married for four months and it had been their first real argument.

It had been a silly argument…trivial. She couldn't even remember what it had been about. In fact at the time she had wondered if Jay had been deliberately winding her up, trying to get a reaction. He'd certainly succeeded. One minute she'd been keeping her cool, the next her temper had erupted and she had felt like throwing something at him. The china figurine in the lounge had been temptingly close to hand.

'You'll be sorry if you do that,' Jay had murmured sardonically as he'd correctly interpreted her intentions.

'Really?' She'd picked up the china anyway. 'How sorry?'

'Very sorry; that's a family heirloom.'

She didn't think she would really have thrown it, but for a few seconds she had been sorely tempted. 'Well, then, maybe you'd better apologise.'

'For what?'

'For being a totally arrogant, irritating, infuriating man.'

He'd taken the statue out of her hand. 'I drive you mad, do I?' His voice had lowered to a husky tone, a tone that had sent her temperature soaring for reasons other than anger.

'Totally.'

He'd reached and kissed her then. The argument had been forgotten. The dinner had been forgotten. Hours later, lying in each other's arms on the settee, they had smelt the acrid fumes of smoke. The Beef Wellington had been charcoal.

And he thought they could just go back to being friends, she thought dryly.

'Sure you don't remember it?' Jay asked again.

'I told you, Jay. I don't remember!' She glared at him, her eyes shimmering with a warning light.

'I think you do,' he said quietly. 'I think you're just frightened to admit it.'

'Rubbish.' She glanced at her watch. 'As dinner is going to be a while longer, I'm going to go and take a shower.'

She moved to go out into the corridor. For a moment she thought he was going to detain her, put a hand on her shoulder. Her heart seemed to thump with a kind of wild anticipation. But he stepped back and allowed her to pass him.

She glanced up at him, her eyes wide, wary. He smiled. 'I've got some paperwork to deal with. I'll be in my study if you need me.'

Perversely she felt disappointed. This was absolutely crazy, she told herself as she headed towards her bedroom. She needed to get Jay Hammond out of her system, stop this wild attraction that she felt for him. Otherwise when she returned to London she was going to be back to how she'd been when she'd first left him...totally and utterly miserable.

She showered and then put on a robe and stood at her bedroom window, looking down at the garden. It was floodlit with lights from the house. But, beyond that, the solitude of the shoreline beckoned.

She felt restless...like a caged lion; she wanted to pace backwards and forwards. The silence of the house was somehow disturbing.

She changed into a fuchsia pink dress and wandered downstairs. The door to Jay's study was closed. She could see the light beneath the door. She wanted to knock and go in. She wanted to tell him that she did remember their argument...and the burnt dinner.

She shook her head, angry with herself, and on impulse she headed outside. Maybe a brisk walk along the beach would help get things in perspective.

It was very warm outside. The sound of insects filled the heaviness of the air with a gentle humming undercurrent. She walked across to the edge of the patio and down the steps to the beach.

There was a full moon shimmering on the velvet darkness of the sea. A breeze whispered in the palm trees. She slipped off her shoes and walked along the edge of the water. It lapped in over her toes, warm like a milky bath.

'You shouldn't be down here in the dark on your own.' The voice from behind her startled her.

'I thought you were working?' She watched as Jay walked over towards her. His face was in shadow, his hair highlighted with silver from the moon.

'I heard you going out.' He caught up with her, then stood behind her, looking out over the sea. 'It's very beautiful down here, isn't it?' he reflected.

'Yes.' She moved back to stand next to him.

'Do you remember the night we made love down here?' he asked in a gentle tone. 'Or have you forgotten that as well?'

She didn't answer. She couldn't lie about that. She felt her chest tighten, felt her heart skip a beat as he reached out and took hold of her hand.

He squeezed it gently. 'I often think about you when I come down here. Think about our first night together.'

'Don't, Jay…' Her voice was a strained whisper.

'Don't what? Remember?' He shook his head, then turned to look at her. 'Do you ever think about those few months we shared as man and wife?'

The husky sexy sound of his voice made her heart stand still. She pulled her hand away from his. 'I…I'd better get back to the house.'

He reached out a hand, tipping her face so that he could look at her. The moonlight made her look very pale; her eyes, a very vivid shade of blue seemed to swamp her face. His gaze moved to her lips.

His fingers moved to brush lightly against them. The tender caress made her ache inside.

'I do,' he said gently. 'We were happy at first, weren't we?'

She felt her eyes mist with tears. 'Yes…I suppose we were.'

She wished she could see him properly, look into his eyes, but he was a blur for a moment. Then he bent his head and his lips brushed lightly against hers. 'I thought it was a pretty good arrangement,' he murmured huskily. 'In fact it was pretty near perfect.'

He kissed her again. The softness of his lips was sweet against hers, sweet and achingly tender.

She forced herself to pull away from him before things could get out of control. Her heart was hammering against her ribs so fiercely she feared they might crack.

'But that's all it was, Jay,' she said unsteadily. 'A suitable arrangement.'

'Yes.' He shrugged. 'But we had a lot going for us. We were friends…we cared about each other—'

'But not enough to sustain a marriage,' she said, thinking about Lisa, about the way he had kissed that woman the night when they'd been alone together working late.

'Have you ever been in love, Elizabeth?' he asked suddenly. 'I mean, deep, all-consuming love?'

'I'm thirty years of age, Jay. Of course I have,' she said briskly. 'In fact I came close to getting married once before when I was in my early twenties.'

'Was he the love of your life?'

The quietly asked question made her frown. She hadn't thought about Daniel in a long time. 'No! I thought he was at the time, but…' she trailed off weakly '…I was mistaken.'

'What happened?'

She shrugged. 'I discovered he was two-timing me and, when I confronted him with it, he admitted it, said he was deeply in love with the other woman and broke it off with me.'

'You've never told me that before.'

She smiled. 'I suppose it's something I don't like to remember. It hurt at the time. But…' she shrugged '…you get over these things, don't you?'

'Sometimes.'

She looked over at him sharply. 'You're over your ex-wife, aren't you?'

'Hell, yes! But it did take time—'

'And a lot of women.' For a second her eyes glimmered with mock humour.

'One woman,' he said softly. 'One woman in particular.'

'Oh, come on, now, Jay.' She stepped back from him. 'You're not going to try and tell me that I helped heal your broken heart…are you?' She shook her head. 'You must think I'm very naive. What is this? Are you trying to charm me into selling out the business?'

'No.' He smiled. 'I'm trying to tell you that…our marriage…our arrangement, as you like to refer to it, worked well. I liked having you around—'

'It was convenient?' She finished for him dryly.

'It was a bit more than that…wasn't it?'

She shook her head and looked out over the sea. 'It just suited you at the time. In case the likes of Lisa Cunningham got too serious.' The derisive words dropped from her lips before she could check them.

'Lisa?' She heard the ominous tone in his voice. 'How do you know about Lisa?'

Her eyes sparkled, over-bright in the moonlight. 'Do you think I'm stupid? Or blind? Or maybe you think I'm both.'

'I don't think you are either,' he said quietly. 'But Lisa was just an affair—'

'I don't really want to know.' She cut across him vehemently, suddenly scared to go on with this conversation.

'Lisa is in the past, Elizabeth.'

'And I said I don't care.'

She turned away from him then and ran across the beach towards the steps.

'Elizabeth, come back.' His voice followed her clearly on the night air. But she wasn't about to comply. She was shaking inside, and she needed to get away from him.

She ran across the lawns, fiercely rubbing the sand from her feet before stepping into her shoes and entering the house by the patio doors.

Jay caught up with her as she crossed the lounge. 'Elizabeth, will you just stop for a moment and let me explain?'

'I don't want you to explain.' She turned around and glared at him. 'What are you going to say? It was just a fling? It didn't mean much? Or she's the love of your life? Whichever it is, I'm not interested. It's not any of my business now.'

'Are you jealous?' he asked suddenly, his tone suddenly quiet, his eyes watchful.

'Not even slightly,' she assured him calmly. While inside there were a million voices screaming, Liar!

'Yes, you are…you're jealous.' He walked closer towards her, a purposeful glint in his eye, a small smile curving his lips.

'I told you, Jay. I couldn't care less. I just want you to know that I won't be misled or bamboozled into selling my shares in the company to you. No matter how charming you are, or how much you say I was the woman who helped you deal with the past.'

'So let's get this straight. You won't sell because of Lisa?'

'No. Watch my lips. I just won't sell.'

'I'm trying not to watch your lips.' He grinned.

'You're impossible.' She turned away from him.

He put a hand on her shoulder and turned her back to face him.

'Lisa was a fling…and it was over a long time ago.'

She stared up at him. For so long she had tried to bury the truth inside her. Tried to blank it out. Talking openly about it only made the hurt worse. 'Well, it doesn't matter now anyway…'

'If it doesn't matter, why bring it up?'

'Just so you know that I won't be fooled, Jay.' She tried to speak in a matter-of-fact tone. 'And I'm very clear-headed where the business is concerned.'

'I'm not trying to fool you.' His voice was deep and gentle.

'Aren't you?' She shook her head. She didn't know if she believed that. She didn't even know if she believed his affair with Lisa was over.

She pulled away from him. 'There's no point talking about this—'

'Of course there is a point. We need to sort things out, Beth.'

'We'll talk in the morning. I'm tired.'

'No, we'll talk now.' He pulled her back. 'How do you know about Lisa?'

'I just do, okay? And I'm not jealous. To be jealous I'd have to give a damn, which I don't. You can see who you want, Jay.' She shrugged.

'And you don't give a damn?'

'No…not one.'

'So I'd be wasting my time asking you to come back, I suppose?'

'Come back?' The fire had gone from her voice now as she stared at him in puzzlement.

'To come back home,' he whispered. 'Give…our "arrangement" another try.'

The shrill ring of the doorbell cut through the silence of the house.

'Who the heck could that be?' Jay glanced at his watch.

'Whoever it is can go away and come back in the morning.'

The bell rang again, a longer more insistent noise.

'You should go and see who it is,' Elizabeth suggested tentatively. 'Maybe it's May and she has forgotten her key.'

Jay shook his head, and then moved away from her. 'Okay, but stay where you are; we need to talk.'

She watched as he left the room.

In a way she was glad of the interruption, it gave her a chance to gather herself together.

He'd said his affair with Lisa was over. She did feel relieved to hear those words…but there was still a lot of pain inside her, a lot of hurt that couldn't be healed just by his telling her the affair was over…and asking would she come back?

Her stomach turned over as she thought about those words. She wanted him so much.

Snippets of their earlier conversation flew through her mind.

'Lisa was a fling…and it was over a long time ago.'

Assuming that he was speaking the truth, did it matter that his affair was over? Did it change anything? He'd still betrayed her…she wasn't sure she could ever forgive that.

Not that he had asked for her forgiveness. Shouldn't he at least have said he was sorry? Even if their union had never been based on declarations of undying love and fidelity, she deserved to be treated with respect.

What was it Jay had said on the beach…? 'Our arrangement, as you like to refer to it, worked well. I liked having you around—'

Did he want her back to act as a buffer for his affairs? The idea was so distasteful that it made her body go cold with abhorrence.

Through the mists of her thoughts she heard her name

being called from the hallway. Frowning, she went to see what was going on.

Jay's voice drifted to her from the front door. He was talking to a woman. Her voice was familiar.

'Cheryl?' She moved further out into the hallway. 'Cheryl, is that you?'

The woman was standing with her back to her, but she turned as she heard Elizabeth's voice.

Her stepmother was an attractive blonde in her late fifties. She had a plump, well-rounded figure, yet was so well-groomed and so stylish that it didn't detract one bit from her loveliness.

Elizabeth's heart leapt with excitement and pleasure as she hurried to greet her.

'Cheryl, we thought you were arriving tomorrow night!'

'Slight change of plan.' Cheryl opened her arms and embraced Beth warmly. 'I can't tell you how good it is to see you.'

'You too.' Elizabeth closed her eyes and held on tightly to the woman who had been a big part of her life when her father had been alive. Then she drew back. 'Where's Alan?' She looked past the woman towards the doorway; there was no one behind her, just one suitcase sitting on the step.

'Ah…that's another story.'

Elizabeth looked back at her stepmother again, noticing for the first time that her eyes were slightly swollen and that behind the wide smile there was a hint of tears.

'Come on,' Elizabeth said briskly. 'I'll put the kettle on and we'll have tea.' She looked over at Jay, about to ask him to carry Cheryl's suitcase inside, but he was already doing it.

'I'm disturbing you,' Cheryl said quickly. 'I don't want to be a bother. Maybe it would be better if I go and we can meet up tomorrow—'

'Don't be silly, you're not disturbing anything.' Elizabeth glanced over and caught the flicker of annoyance in Jay's eyes as he put the suitcase down.

'I wasn't even sure I'd find you here. I was going to go to the hotel and ring you in the morning—' Cheryl said distractedly as Elizabeth led her through to the kitchen. 'I should have done.'

'No. You've done the right thing coming here,' Elizabeth said firmly. She put the kettle on and then turned to look at the other woman. 'What's wrong?' she asked gently, and was completely horrified when Cheryl broke down into copious floods of tears.

'What is it?' Elizabeth went across and put her arms around the woman.

'Alan and I had a terrible row,' Cheryl murmured brokenly in between sobs.

'A lovers' tiff?' Elizabeth suggested gently.

'No...' Cheryl pulled away from her. 'It's more than that. We've called the wedding off.'

'Oh, Cheryl! Why?'

The woman shook her head and pulled a chair out to sit down at the kitchen table. 'Because I wanted to get married out here...he said I was still in love with your father...that I was trying to recapture the past.' Cheryl buried her head in her hands for a while.

'But you're not, are you?'

'I don't know. When he said it, suddenly even I wasn't sure. It's only been eighteen months since your father died...maybe Alan is right.'

Jay came in and looked from one to the other. 'I put Cheryl's case upstairs in the spare room at the end of the landing.'

Elizabeth nodded, her eyes full of gratitude; they couldn't let Cheryl go to a hotel in this state.

'I've got to go out,' Jay said quietly. He glanced over at Cheryl. 'See you later, okay?'

'Very diplomatic,' Cheryl said, glancing over at him. 'Thanks, Jay…I really appreciate this.'

'No problem.' Jay said easily. Across the kitchen his eyes met with Elizabeth's. 'We'll talk later, okay?'

She nodded.

As they were left alone, Cheryl looked over at Elizabeth with a raised brow. 'Well, at least you two seem to be all right again. That's one weight off my mind. I was so upset when you told me you'd split up.'

Elizabeth shrugged.

'You are back together again?' Cheryl asked.

'I don't think so.' Elizabeth sighed. 'It's a long story, Cheryl. But I think you know that our marriage was never based on love to begin with. And when you haven't got that…well, there's not much chance for a relationship surviving, is there?'

Jay had left his wallet on the kitchen table. He'd been in the process of turning back for it when he'd heard Elizabeth's words clearly through the door. They had made him stop in his tracks.

'Hell…' Cheryl pulled a face. 'Have you got any chocolate in the house?' she asked suddenly.

Elizabeth smiled. 'I don't know. But there is a joint of meat in the oven if you're hungry?'

Outside the door, Jay turned away. He felt in need of something a bit stronger than chocolate, he thought as he headed for the front door.

Elizabeth lay in bed and watched the early-morning sunrise outside her window. She wondered what time Jay had got back in last night. She knew he had been giving Cheryl space and privacy to talk about her relationship breaking up, but she had hoped that he would return early enough for them to talk. It had been midnight when Cheryl had retired for the night, and there had still been no sign of Jay.

Elizabeth got out of bed and went through to the bathroom to shower. She didn't feel very well, probably because she'd hardly slept last night. She'd been going over and over Jay's words.

Had he been serious when he'd suggested she came back? The words had fallen so nonchalantly from his lips it had been hard to tell.

And if he was serious? She didn't know what to think.

She dressed in a pale yellow sundress and applied some lipstick to brighten herself up. Then went downstairs to make a drink.

She was surprised to find Cheryl, fully dressed and sitting in the kitchen.

'Couldn't you sleep either?' She asked gently as she sat down beside her.

Cheryl shook her head. 'What am I going to do, Beth?'

'Do you love him?'

'I thought I did.'

Elizabeth sighed. 'You know it could just be a case of pre-wedding nerves.'

'Yes, it could. I have to admit I am scared. And maybe he is too. I was lying last night thinking over everything. And you know the main reason I wanted to get married over here was because of you...Elizabeth. You're the only family I've got and I don't think I realised just how important that was until I started to think about the wedding.'

Elizabeth reached and covered Cheryl's hand with her own. 'You should ring Alan and talk to him.'

Cheryl nodded. 'That's what I'll do.' She smiled at Elizabeth. 'So, what about you and Jay?'

'Now that is the hundred-million-dollar question.'

'You should ask him to tell you everything about Lisa

Cunningham,' Cheryl said briskly. 'When they met, when the affair started and finished…everything…'

'I know.' Elizabeth nodded. 'Trouble is, just the mention of her name makes me break out in a panic. I've wanted to ask him for so long, but I'm terrified. Plus I don't want to fling accusations at him. I've tried to wait for the right time, tried to find a calm and reasonable tone to start the conversation…' Elizabeth shook her head. 'But as soon as I even think her name, the words "reasonable" and "calm" seem another world away. And I end up saying nothing—or, like last night, anger erupts inside me.'

The kettle boiled and Elizabeth stood up to make the tea.

'Plus I worry about the fact that even if he has finished with her…there'd be someone else to take her place.'

'Yes…you.'

Elizabeth turned around and looked at her stepmother with a rueful smile. 'I'd give anything to believe that.'

'Have you got anything to lose by not giving it another go?'

Elizabeth poured them both a drink, and suddenly her hand wasn't entirely steady. What she wasn't telling her stepmother was that she thought she might be pregnant.

For a moment she imagined herself back in her apartment in London as a single mother. Could she cope on her own?

She imagined a toddler, perhaps a little boy who looked like his dad, with dark hair and dark eyes. She'd call him Alex…yes, Alex was a nice name.

Wouldn't it be so much better to bring him up here, with his father?

She snapped out of the daydream and glanced at her watch. She was being ridiculous. She probably wasn't pregnant at all.

'Jay is going to be late for the yard,' she murmured. 'I wonder, has he slept in?'

'He left about an hour ago,' Cheryl said. 'He told me to tell you that your car is still in the garage and it's fine to drive. The keys are on the hook behind the door.'

'Oh.' Elizabeth put the cups down on the table. 'How about if we go and do some shopping?' she suggested suddenly.

'Retail therapy…good idea.' Cheryl nodded. 'Then I'd better go over to the hotel. We were supposed to be checking in tonight…I'll have to tell them the wedding is off.'

Elizabeth looked over at her stepmother with sympathy. 'I can feel a major shopping expedition coming on.'

Burying himself in work didn't seem to help. By late afternoon Jay had had enough. He packed up, turned off the computer and headed out of the office.

He was disappointed when he got home to find the house empty. For a while he paced around, not knowing what to do with himself. He phoned May to see how her daughter-in-law was doing and was relieved to be told that the fall hadn't been serious. Both mother and baby were unharmed. But then Jay returned to his pacing, every now and then glancing out towards the drive, hoping that Elizabeth's car would pull up outside.

After an hour of this, he went into the study and turned on the computer in there, desperately trying to take his mind off things by working. But all he could think about was Elizabeth. Her words to Cheryl about their marriage not being based on love, and therefore having no chance of survival, had brought home harsh reality.

When he finally heard the sound of the car engine it was starting to go dark. He didn't move from the computer, but his study door was ajar and he could see the front hallway. He waited for the sound of the door opening.

'It's absolutely wonderful, Cheryl.'

He heard Elizabeth's animated tones first.

Then the lights flicked on in the hallway. 'You must feel happy now, surely?'

He saw Elizabeth putting down several carrier bags.

'I can't tell you how I feel,' Cheryl was saying. 'I didn't realise just how much I loved him until I saw him standing there.'

'Saw who, standing where?' Jay switched on the light beside his desk and Elizabeth turned in surprise.

'Jay! I didn't see you.' She came over and pushed his study door open further. 'We went over to the hotel to cancel Cheryl's booking and Alan...her fiancé was there.'

'Really?' Jay smiled. 'Well, that's good news.'

'Yes.' Elizabeth beamed at him, her eyes lit with excitement. 'It was all very romantic, they fell into each other's arms in Reception.'

'He'd followed me to declare his everlasting love,' Cheryl said with a hint of self-effacing amusement in her voice.

'Does this mean the wedding is back on?' Jay asked casually.

'Certainly does.' Cheryl's smile seemed to reach from ear to ear. 'Thank you so much for putting up with me, Jay. I really appreciated your help.'

'I didn't do anything.' Jay glanced over at Elizabeth, thinking how radiant she looked, how happy. She'd no right to look like that, he thought suddenly. Not when he felt like hell.

'You did more than you'll ever know,' Cheryl said seriously. 'Letting me stay here. Spending time with Elizabeth helped so much.'

Jay shrugged. 'Elizabeth has that effect. Her father always said she was good in a crisis. A kind of Pollyanna for broken hearts.' He added dryly.

'Yes...' Cheryl sounded a bit hesitant now.

As well she might, Elizabeth thought with annoyance. What the heck did he mean by that? She met the coolness of his dark eyes and felt the pleasure she had derived from Cheryl's happiness start to melt.

'Well, I'll go and get my things together,' Cheryl said, flicking a look over at her stepdaughter. 'Alan will be waiting for me back at the hotel. And I know you two have got things to sort out.'

As she hurried away from them up the stairs Elizabeth felt apprehension settle over her like a dark blanket.

The way Jay was looking at her was a million miles away from the way he had looked at her last night on the beach. He seemed so distant, so cold.

For a moment the silence between them seemed strained to the point of unbearable. 'I suppose you want to go to the hotel as well?' Jay said suddenly.

The words hit her like a body-blow. 'I suppose I should.' Her voice sounded most unlike herself. She'd made no plans to leave with Cheryl. In fact during the day she had started to think in more positive terms about her relationship with Jay. She had looked forward to seeing him this evening. Had told herself that they needed to talk honestly, openly.

What a joke, she thought now. Obviously he hadn't been serious about them giving the relationship another chance.

'I thought things over last night.' Jay shrugged. 'And maybe you're right. There's no point in us trying again...we're better off to stay as friends.'

'Yes.' She didn't know what else to say.

'Good news,' Jay said suddenly. 'You must have done a good job convincing our bank manager of your commitment to the business. The bank has said okay to our loan.' He pulled out a drawer and took out some papers. 'The paperwork arrived this morning by special delivery.'

'You must be pleased.'

'Yes.' He slid the papers towards her. 'You may as well take them and read them. If you have any questions you can ask George at our meeting tomorrow. If not, you can just sign them and give them back to me. That way there's probably no need for you to come to the bank with me at all.' He shrugged. 'It's up to you.'

She walked across to his desk and picked up the papers. Was this why he was acting so cool towards her now? He thought he'd gone about as far with her as he could go, both in bed and business, and this was the end of the line?

She felt sick inside.

'I'll read them and get back to you,' she murmured, avoiding meeting his eye.

'Yes, you do that.'

She turned away and left the room, closing the door firmly behind her and hurrying upstairs.

'Beth, is that you?' Cheryl popped her head out from her bedroom. 'Do you think you could ring a taxi for me?'

'No need,' Elizabeth said as she went into her own room. 'I'm coming with you.'

She started to throw things into her case, anger fuelling her movements. How could she have been so stupid as to even hope for one minute that things could be different between them? she thought furiously. How could she make the same mistake again?

Some people never learnt.

'Elizabeth?' She turned at Cheryl's voice in the hallway. 'Are you all right?'

'No.' Elizabeth threw the last item of clothing in the case and snapped it closed. 'But the sooner I get out of here, the sooner I'll feel better.'

Jay didn't come out of his study until he had heard the front door close behind them. Then he walked through to the hall. The first thing he noticed was the shopping bags on the floor. With a frown he went to pick them up.

They were full of groceries. He carried them through to the kitchen and started to unpack them. If Elizabeth had bought groceries, did that mean she'd had no intention of leaving with Cheryl to go to the hotel? The question crept unwanted into his head. If he hadn't pushed her, would she have stayed?

Maybe she would, but for how long? A couple of days at most, he told himself furiously. What the hell was the point? Their marriage was over. He might be able to turn her on in the bedroom, but he couldn't make her happy outside of it.

He finished unpacking one bag and reached for the next, only to find it full of ladies' toiletries and, at the very top, staring at him, a pregnancy testing kit.

CHAPTER TEN

IT WAS one of the top hotels in Jamaica and it seemed to be full of couples in love. Even worse was the fact that every time Elizabeth walked past the reception and out towards the beach she was reminded of her own wedding day.

Of all the places to end up staying, she thought bleakly. This had to be the ultimate in self-punishment.

She sat with Cheryl on the terrace, trying to eat breakfast. But she wasn't hungry. She had to meet Jay at the bank this morning, and she wasn't looking forward to it.

He'd rung early to ask if she wanted him to pick her up, or collect the papers. The sound of his voice had made her want to cry. She'd been very abrupt, had just said no, thank you, and put the phone down.

'You okay?' Cheryl leaned across and asked gently.

'Yes, fine. Just full of apprehension.' Elizabeth took a deep breath. 'I've made a decision about the yard. I'm going to sell to Jay.'

'Elizabeth!' Cheryl looked shocked.

'I should never, ever have gone along with that daft will of my father's in the first place,' Elizabeth said shakily. 'I was asking for trouble.'

Cheryl smiled. 'Henry always did have a wacky sense of humour. But I'll tell you something now.' She leaned forward. 'He told me what he was going to do when he made that will out. He hoped it would push you two together.'

'Well, it didn't.' Elizabeth shrugged. 'It was a disaster.'

'Henry asked if it didn't work out and you didn't marry

155

Jay, would I give you the yard anyway. He said that it belonged by rights to you, Beth, and I agreed.'

'Yes…I know.' Elizabeth's eyes misted with tears. 'You told me that on the day of the funeral.'

'Did I? I can't remember much about the funeral; it's all a terrible blur now,' Cheryl said bleakly.

'Well you did. And I asked you not to mention that fact to Jay.' For a moment Elizabeth closed her eyes on the brightness of the day. 'To all intents and purposes, I conned him into marrying me.'

'He didn't have to accept your proposal, though, did he?' Cheryl said. 'You've got nothing to reproach yourself for.'

'No. So why do I feel as if I do?' Elizabeth opened her eyes and shook her head. 'Dad knew the yard wouldn't really be worth anything without Jay working there. Which was probably another reason for him trying to push us together.' She looked away from Cheryl. 'Anyway, it's too late for recriminations. That's why I'm going to sell my shares in the company to Jay, cut my losses and run. He deserves to have the business; he's worked very hard building it up.' Across the terrace she saw Cheryl's fiancé approaching.

Alan was a handsome man in his early sixties, and Elizabeth had genuinely liked him from the moment they'd met. She was glad that he and Cheryl seemed to have resolved their differences. 'Let's not talk about this any more, Cheryl,' she said quickly. 'We need to put the past behind us and concentrate on the future now.'

The appointment at the bank was for eleven-thirty. Elizabeth arrived a few minutes early and was asked to wait in the reception area. She flicked through a few magazines on the coffee table and tried to pretend that she was relaxed and wasn't watching for Jay to appear from the lifts opposite.

However, when the doors opened and he strolled in, exactly on time she felt her nerves flutter with apprehension.

He looked cool and relaxed in a light-coloured pair of trousers and an open-necked shirt with the sleeves rolled up. His eyes met with hers and he smiled. 'Hi, have you been waiting long?'

She shook her head, not trusting herself to speak.

He sat down next to her on the settee. 'How are Cheryl and Alan this morning?' he asked nonchalantly.

'Fine.' She flicked over the pages of the glossy magazine. For a moment the only sound was the whirr of the air-conditioning unit.

His gaze travelled from the high heels she wore, up over the long shapely length of her legs, to her trim figure. She was wearing a powder-blue dress; it was smart and plain yet, on her, somehow tremendously sexy.

'And are you okay?' he asked gently into the silence.

'Fine.' She flicked over another couple of pages.

He frowned. 'You had a phone call from London last night,' he said suddenly.

He noticed how that gained her full attention. She looked at him, her blue eyes wide and questioning.

'Someone called Colin,' Jay enlightened her. 'He said could you phone him at the office today?'

'Right.' She smiled, a look of pleasure lighting her eyes for just a second, before she returned her attention to the magazine.

'Obviously they can't do without you back there,' Jay murmured.

'Colin probably just needs to ask me something about the account,' she murmured.

Jay's eyes flicked towards the clock on the wall. He'd

been trying to remember which one Colin was. For a while last night he had been mentally going over the guest list at Elizabeth's party, trying to put a face to him. But did it matter? he asked himself now. If she was seeing John or Colin, or Tom, Dick or Harry, it didn't really make any difference. The bottom line was she would be going back to London, into someone else's arms.

'Did you sign the papers?' he asked gruffly.

She glanced over at him. 'Why do I get this funny feeling of *déjà vu*?' she muttered sardonically.

'So you have signed the papers for the loan?'

She felt her cheeks colour red. 'No…not exactly.'

He frowned. 'I think I'm the one experiencing *déjà vu*.'

The office door opened and George came out. 'I'm very sorry to keep you waiting.' He smiled at them both and reached to shake their hands as they stood up. 'Did you get the papers I sent?' he asked, turning to lead the way back into his office.

'We did indeed.' Jay held a chair for Elizabeth before sitting down next to her opposite the bank manager.

'And is everything to your satisfaction?' George asked, his smile wide and enthusiastic as he settled himself behind his desk.

'Well, it is as far as I'm concerned.' Jay glanced across at Elizabeth. 'But I think my wife has a few reservations.'

'Oh?' George fixed Elizabeth with a look of enquiry. 'What's the problem?'

The problem was that when Jay referred to her as his wife, it gave her a shivery, warm feeling inside. It confused her senses totally. 'There's no problem as such.' She kept her voice low and tried to inject confidence into it. Tried to tell herself that she was doing the right thing. 'It's just that I've decided to sell my share in the business after all.'

There was silence in the room.

'I see.' George looked surprised.

She didn't even dare glance at Jay. Because if he looked too pleased it would completely throw her off balance, and she couldn't afford for that to happen.

'Well that puts a whole different perspective on things.' George said. He was riffling through the file of papers on his desk. 'So have you accepted the terms of Jay's original offer?'

'Yes.' Elizabeth reached into her bag and brought out the papers that Jay had sent to her in London. 'I signed them last night.' She put the envelope down on the desk.

'Good.' George nodded and reached to pick them up.

'Not so fast.' Jay's hand got there first and he was the one picking up the envelope. 'I'd like to look this over first, if you don't mind George?'

'No. Of course not.'

Elizabeth frowned and glanced over at Jay. 'What is there to look over? It's the offer you made. The one you were so keen for me to sign in London.'

'I know what it is, Beth.' His dark eyes seemed to bore right into her. 'But I need to look at it again.'

Elizabeth didn't answer him. She was staring at him in perplexity.

'Well, it's a big decision,' George murmured soothingly. 'Perhaps you should both go away, have lunch and discuss it.' He flicked over his desk diary. 'I can see you again this day next week, if that's a help?'

'Not really.' Elizabeth murmured. 'I've booked my return flight to London for Sunday morning—'

'Just pencil me into your diary for next week,' Jay said abruptly, pushing his chair back. 'We'll discuss things further then.'

George nodded. 'Very well…'

'Thanks a lot, George.' Jay shook hands with the other man. 'I appreciate your assistance.' Then, before she could gather her thoughts properly, he was steering Elizabeth out of the office.

'What on earth is all the hurry?' she muttered angrily, as he marched her towards the lifts, his hand still firmly on her arm.

Jay didn't answer her until the lift doors opened and they had stepped inside, away from prying eyes.

'What the hell did you think you were playing at in there?' he grated, his tone raw with fury.

'Why are you looking at me like that? Isn't this what you wanted?' She glared at him. 'You can have the business. I'm stepping out of the ring.'

'You don't believe in discussing things, do you, Beth?' He was furious. His eyes cold and harshly condemning as they raked over her. 'We are supposed to be presenting a united front to the bank. Couldn't you at least have dropped me a clue as to what you were going to do today?'

She shrugged. 'Does it matter any more? I'm selling out to you; we don't need to pretend to the bank…do we?'

'So you don't think you even owed me a premonitory hint as to what you were planning?'

'Not really. It's my decision to make…and I've made it.'

The lift doors opened and she marched out ahead of him, through the small foyer and out into the street. The sunshine was blinding after the darkness of the bank, the heat intense.

She kept up a brisk walk towards where she had parked her car. Jay walked with her. 'So there's nothing more you want to discuss?'

'Not really.' She didn't glance sideways at him.

They walked past the local market. The stalls were laden with fresh fruit and vegetables. It was a colourful, bustling place, alive with people. Stall holders called out to them as they passed, eager for them to try their produce. The smell of fruit mixed with the smell of fresh fish on the neighbouring stalls. The odour was pungent in the searing heat.

All of a sudden, Elizabeth didn't feel very well. She really needed to slow down. Walking this fast in the midday sun wasn't a good idea. But she wanted to get away from Jay, so she didn't pay any attention to the warning lights that were flashing inside.

They passed the market and the pavement narrowed. Jay walked on the road beside her.

'Where have you parked?' she asked, wondering if he was following her, or if he had been heading in this direction anyway.

'Further down here.' He put out a hand, stopping her, as they reached a busy junction. 'Be careful,' he said warningly as a car screeched around the corner past them.

'I'm capable of crossing a road, Jay,' she said, trying to shrug his hand away from her arm.

He threw her a measured glance, and kept his hand where it was.

'So what's made you suddenly decide to sell out to me?' he asked.

'I thought about it and you're right. There's no point in my holding onto a business when my life is in London now.'

His hand moved from her arm. 'I see.'

The way was clear and she started to cross over. The heat seemed to be so powerful that it was melting the road. The smell of hot bitumen assailed her senses.

'I don't know why you are so annoyed with me,' she said furiously. 'This is what you want. You'll have complete control of the yard.' She felt dizzy now and she slowed her footsteps, suddenly scared that she was going to pass out right here in the middle of the road.

'I don't know what the hell I want, but it would have

been nice to have been forewarned before going in there today.' Jay frowned as he looked at her. 'Are you okay?'

'Fine.' She had reached her car and was scrabbling inside her purse, looking for her keys.

'You don't look it.'

'Thanks,' she grated sardonically. Why couldn't she find her keys? It felt as if it was a hundred and ten in the shade. The pavement seemed to be moving under her feet, yet she was standing still. It was a weird and disorientating feeling. She fought down a wave of sickness. 'Perhaps you could just go away and leave me on my own?' she said, her voice laced with sudden panic. She didn't want him to see her like this.

'I don't think so.' His arm went around her waist, something she was intensely grateful for a second later as her legs didn't seem to want to support her any more. She leaned against him.

'I don't feel very well,' she admitted softly.

'You'll be okay.' His voice was gentle now, and a far cry from a few moments ago. 'Take a few deep breaths.' His arm was still reassuringly around her.

'I can't. It's so hot.' She wondered if people were looking at them as they passed in the street.

'My Jeep is just behind your car.' Jay's voice was sympathetic against her ear. 'Come on. I'll drive you back.'

She wanted to argue, wanted to tell him to go away, but she didn't dare. She didn't want to be left here, feeling like this. She felt incredibly vulnerable, unbelievably weak. It was a dreadful feeling.

She allowed him to help her towards his Jeep.

'Feel any better?' he asked as he opened the passenger door and she sat down.

Now that she was sitting down she did. She nodded, feeling foolish. 'Just let me get my breath. I'll probably be fine in a few minutes and able to drive myself back to the hotel.'

Jay cast her a sceptical look, then closed the door on her and went around to the driver's side.

He turned on the engine so that the air-conditioning sprang to life. The relief was instant. 'Sorry about that,' she murmured, leaning her head back against the seat. 'It was just the heat, I think.'

Jay didn't say anything, his gaze was raking over her. He'd never seen her quite so pale. Her skin had a bluish tinge, as if her dress was reflected on it. Her eyes seemed to dominate her face, sea-blue with dark smudges beneath.

'I guess I'm not used to these temperatures any more,' she reiterated, trying to break the sudden feeling of tension.

'I'll take you back to the hotel,' he said quietly.

She opened her mouth to argue and he glanced at her sharply. She knew him well enough to know that look brooked absolutely no argument. Maybe he was right, she thought abruptly. She wasn't in a fit state to drive. So, she acceded gracefully. 'Thanks, I'd appreciate the lift.'

A small derisive smile curved the corners of his mouth. Then he turned his attention to the road, pulling out into the traffic when there was a space.

She frowned and looked out at the passing scenery. She felt a lot better than she had, but in truth she still felt a bit spaced out.

Was she pregnant? The question sent a ripple of fear through her. What would she do if she found she was? Would she cope alone?

'How's May's daughter-in-law?' she asked, trying very hard to turn her mind away from herself.

'The baby is fine and they've let her out of hospital, but she has to take it easy. May's staying over there to look after things.'

'Well that's good news.'

'Yes…' he agreed heavily. 'Something that's a bit short on the ground about now.'

She frowned. 'Isn't it good news that I've decided to sell to you?' she said. 'I honestly thought you'd be pleased.'

'I am, I suppose,' he muttered.

'It doesn't sound like you are.' She looked over at him, her heart racing; she felt confused by his reaction to her news. Confused, scared—a little hopeful in a perversely persistent way.

'I told you, I think you should have pre-warned me about what you wanted to do. I felt liked a damned idiot in that bank, as if I didn't have any idea what my own wife wanted.'

'You mean I dented your pride,' Elizabeth grated, her temper rising again. She should have known that was all he would be bothered about. 'But look at it this way, it's just a minor irritation. I've signed your papers and I'll be out of your hair next week.'

He made no reply, just turned the Jeep through the gates leading to her hotel.

'Drop me at the front entrance. I'll be fine from there,' she said, wanting to get away from this situation and from him. She felt like crying, and that would be a disaster. She'd already made enough of a fool of herself around Jay Hammond.

He ignored her and parked in the car park. 'I'll come in with you,' he said.

'No…really, I'm fine now.'

But she was talking to herself. He was already out of the Jeep and coming around to open her door for her.

She got out herself, before he could offer her his hand.

'You must have a busy afternoon ahead of you at the yard,' she said hastily. 'Thanks for the lift, but I won't detain you further.'

He took hold of her, one arm firmly around her waist. 'I've got time to come in with you,' he said firmly.

Short of starting an argument, Elizabeth could do little but comply.

She noticed that he had taken his jacket out from the back of the Jeep and was carrying it over one arm.

Was he concerned about getting cold? If so, there had to be something seriously wrong with her. She felt that, if she stood still long enough out here, she might fry.

They walked through Reception and out past the terrace. 'My room is just down here,' she said, pointing towards the path that led through the gardens by the side of the beach.

'Okay.' One arm still firmly at her back, he walked with her.

'I feel a lot better now.' she said, opening her purse to look for her room key 'And I'm sure you've got things to do.'

He smiled. 'I've nothing to do.'

'Aren't you going in to the yard today?'

'What do you care?' he asked suddenly. 'As you're selling it, it doesn't really matter if the whole place falls apart, does it?'

'Well…I wouldn't like to think it will fall apart…' She found the key, her fingers closing around it gratefully.

'My room is here.' She stepped across the lawn towards one of the hexagonal-shaped beach bungalows. With its quaint thatch roof and whitewashed walls, it looked like a designer honeypot.

Jay took the key from her and unlocked the door.

'Well, goodbye—'

'I'm not going anywhere yet.' He stepped inside with her.

A large fan whirred from wooden rafters inside the cylindrical vertex of the ceiling, making the room blissfully cool.

'I'd forgotten how pretty these rooms are,' Jay said, his gaze sweeping over the enormous bed covered with bright blue and yellow covers, then out towards the view from the window of the turquoise Caribbean.

'Yes, they're nice.' Elizabeth's heels clicked on the tiled floor as she crossed to pour herself a glass of water from the jug on the dressing table. 'Would you like a drink?' she asked politely, feeling obliged to offer.

'No, thanks.'

She took her glass of water and sat on the edge of the bed.

'At least you've got some colour back in your face,' he remarked.

'Yes, I feel much better now, thank you.' She wished he would take the hint and go. She wanted to lie down. Although she felt better, she didn't feel one hundred per cent.

'What room number is Cheryl in?' Jay asked, going over to the phone on the bedside table. 'I'll ring and see if she's there.'

'Why?'

'I would have thought that was obvious. I don't want to leave you on your own when you're not well.'

'I told you, I'm fine now, Jay,' she said quickly. 'There's no need for fuss—'

'I think there is.' He fixed her with a steady, level gaze. 'So which room is she in, or do I have to phone Reception to ask?'

Elizabeth glared at him. 'Room seventy,' she said grudgingly.

He picked up the phone and dialled the room. After a while, when there was no answer, he dialled through to Reception and asked for her to be paged.

'Okay, now you can go,' Elizabeth said briskly as he put the phone back down.

His eyes moved over her. 'I think you should lie down,' he said suddenly. 'You nearly fainted, Beth, you need to take it easy for a while.'

'Yes…and I will…after you go.'

'I'm not going anywhere until Cheryl gets here. In fact I'm in two minds whether or not to ring my doctor and ask him to come down here and examine you.'

'You are joking!' Her eyes widened in horror.

'I don't really think it's a joking matter, do you?' His eyes were steely as they rested on her. 'You're pregnant, aren't you?' he asked calmly.

'No…' She felt her face suffuse with colour.

'Don't lie to me, Elizabeth.' He wouldn't release her eyes, holding them with an intense look that made her feel as if he could see right inside her. 'You've lived in this country for years and I've never seen the heat affect you the way it has today.'

'I told you, I'm not acclimatised to it, that's all.' She shrugged, trying to make light of the episode, trying to sound convincing. But her words rang hollowly in the room. She could tell that he wasn't at all convinced. And, as she wasn't convinced herself, who could blame him? she thought wryly.

'So you don't need this, then?' He put down his jacket and held up the pregnancy testing kit she had bought yesterday as if it were an exhibit in a court-room trial.

She was horrified, both by the fact that he had found it amongst her shopping and that he had the audacity to bring it here and confront her like this.

Well?' The dark eyes seemed to burn into her.

She didn't answer.

'Just give me a straight answer, Beth. Are you pregnant?'

'If I knew that, I wouldn't have bought that kit, would I?' She glared up at him, her eyes fierce. 'Just stop asking me, all right?'

'No, it's not all right,' he said quietly. 'How late are you?'

She stood up and paced nervously towards the window. 'Just go away.'

'No, I won't damn well go away.'

Her breath was catching painfully against her chest. She watched the surf rolling in against the white beach below them and tried to think calming thoughts. But nothing would come to her. All she could think was that she loved Jay with all her heart and she would probably never get over the fact that he just couldn't return those feelings.

He threw the box down on the bed behind her. 'Why ever did you agree to the terms of our marriage when you really had no feelings for me?' he asked suddenly.

The mocking question made her go hot inside. 'You know why I agreed. I wanted what was rightfully mine. My father's boat yard.'

'So it was just the money?'

'No!' She spun around to face him, the denial breaking from her lips without her being aware that she had uttered it.

'So what was it?'

'It was…' She stared at him wordlessly. She couldn't tell him it was because she had loved him. She had her pride. 'It was just a matter of principle. The yard should rightfully have been mine.'

He laughed at that. 'It's rich hearing you talk about principles. Don't you think you sacrificed all of those when you suggested a marriage for purely business reasons? Then proceeded to share my bed?'

She looked away from him.

'Don't lecture me, Jay. You were the one who insisted

that the marriage be a real one. You said you wouldn't go through with it if it were in name only. You made me sign a premarital contract. They were your terms.'

'Yes, they were, and you reneged on the deal.'

'No, I didn't. I slept with you.' Her voice trembled alarmingly.

'Suffered my advances, you mean?'

She looked back at him sharply. 'You know that's not true.'

'No.... Sex was one department where we were always compatible...wasn't it?' His voice was low, the look in his eyes intense.

She felt her body burn with heat.

'Pity that was all we had going for us,' Jay continued softly. 'But never mind. I did enjoy our little interludes together.'

'Don't talk about what we shared together like that,' she warned him shakily.

'Why not?' His voice was calm.

She hated him in that second, hated that he could trivial-ise what they had shared, turn something so special and precious into a meaningless fling.

'So, tell me,' he murmured when she made no attempt to answer him, 'what do you think the chances are that the baby will be mine?'

Red-hot temper seared through her at those words. She raised her hand and swung it back, the urge to slap him acutely intense. Before she could make contact, however, he caught hold of her wrist.

'I wouldn't do that if I were you,' he warned in a low tone.

Her eyes locked with his, her temper instantly evapo-rating. She stared at him, horrified by what she had so nearly done. 'I'm sorry.' She whispered the words in a trembling tone. 'I didn't mean to do that.'

He just stared at her calmly, his eyes dark and intense. Then he let go of her hand. 'No, I'm sorry,' he said gently. 'I shouldn't have said what I did. But I just want you to give me a straight answer for once.'

Her eyes brimmed with sudden tears. 'If I'm pregnant then the baby is yours.' She whispered the words unsteadily. 'It has to be yours…because there's been nobody else.'

He watched as a tear rolled unashamedly down the pallor of her skin.

'You led me to believe—'

'Because I wanted you to know that you're not a supreme being, Jay Hammond,' she told him shakily. 'I've had plenty of offers from men since we've been apart…and before we got married, for that matter—'

'Hell…Elizabeth, I know that. I'm not blind. I see the way men look at you.'

'Yes, well…I just wanted you to know that I don't need you.' She angled her chin up defiantly, a look that was at complete odds with the tears rolling down her cheeks. 'In fact I can manage very well on my own.'

'I know…I bloody well wish you couldn't.' His voice was raw suddenly. 'You're too damn capable.'

'No, I'm not.' She sniffed, and wiped the tears away from her face with a trembling hand. 'If you really want to know, I'm scared stiff.'

'What of?' he asked quietly.

'Of being pregnant and being on my own…'

'Oh, Beth…' Suddenly she was folded into his arms and held tightly against the warmth of his chest. 'You don't have to be on your own.'

'Yes, I do.' Despite the words, she allowed herself to relax against him, trying to steady herself, trying to think logically.

It was bliss to be in his arms; she just wished she could stop thinking. Forget the fact that he didn't love her. Forget everything except the fact that she loved him and this was where she wanted to be more than anything in the world.

'I'll look after you—' he murmured gently, stroking her hair back from her face and gently kissing away the tears on the softness of her skin.

'I don't want you to look after me.' Fiercely she pulled away from him. 'I don't need or want your charity.'

She turned her back on him.

'I'm not offering you charity, Elizabeth. That's absurd.'

'Whatever you're offering, it isn't enough,' she told him shakily.

There was a long silence. In it, Elizabeth strove to get herself back under control. 'I think you had better go now,' she whispered softly.

'So you're not seeing anyone else in London?' he asked, totally ignoring her request.

She shook her head.

'I don't understand why you lied,' he muttered angrily. 'I thought...no...I was convinced you were dating your boss. I saw you with him the day after we slept together. I came to the office. I wanted to take you out for lunch, but you were with him.'

'He's my boss, we often have a working lunch.' She shrugged and walked away to get herself a tissue from her handbag.

He watched the way her hands trembled as she opened the bag.

'I just can't understand why you lied about the fact you were seeing someone seriously.'

'I told you I wasn't dating John,' she said firmly. 'The very idea is preposterous. He's happily married.'

'But you let me think there was someone else,' he persisted.

'I told you why.' She wiped her eyes and glared at him

across the room. 'It was a white lie. I said it in the heat of the moment. To make you go…'

'And you still want me to go?'

She shrugged. In truth she didn't know what she wanted. If she could make him love her, make him be the man she wanted him to be…she'd fling caution and pride away. But what was the point? Even if he took her back, she'd always be watching him, knowing he didn't really love her. And worrying that maybe the next beautiful woman who cast her gaze on him would be the one to win him. That was no way to live her life.

'If you're pregnant, will you stay?'

She looked over at him with a raised eyebrow. 'Don't tell me you fancy being a father?'

'The thought isn't unappealing,' he said calmly. 'I think I'd make a good dad.'

'You probably would,' she said stiffly. 'But a baby isn't a good enough reason to stay together.'

'If you're pregnant, I don't want you to go back to London,' he said tersely.

'That's not your decision to make,' she said quietly. 'It's mine.'

'I suppose it is.' He shook his head. 'But it shouldn't be…it should be a decision we make together.'

'It's all hypothetical anyway.' She tried to shrug off the dilemma. 'I felt a bit dizzy, that's all. Probably it's just a case of too much sun.'

'Well, let's find out, shall we?' Jay nodded his head calmly in the direction of the kit on the bed. 'Why don't you go into the bathroom and use that?'

'I will not!' She was appalled.

He crossed towards the phone and lifted the receiver.

'What are you doing?' she asked, her voice rising.

'Phoning my doctor.' He was punching out numbers on the dial, a look of grim resolution on his face.

'Don't!' She went over towards him and tried to take the receiver out of his hand, but he held it out of her way and finished dialling.

'Hi, Jayne? This is Jay Hammond.'

Appalled, Elizabeth tried to get to the phone so that she could cut him off. But Jay caught hold of her, holding her back with a nonchalant ease. 'Yes. I want to make an appointment for my wife to see the doctor today. In fact, I'd appreciate it if you could fit her in as soon as possible—'

Elizabeth struggled in vain to get free of his hand so that she could take the receiver away from him, but it was like a mouse struggling with a cat. She was using all her strength while he was expending none.

'All right...I'll use the kit,' she said, panic-stricken. 'Just put the phone down.'

'Hold on a minute, Jayne.' Jay covered the mouthpiece. 'Is that a promise?' he asked Elizabeth in a low tone that was somehow very ominous.

She nodded angrily.

'I'll have to get back to you on that, Jayne,' he said, returning his attention to the receptionist on the phone. 'Yes...I will. Bye, now.' He put the phone down and stared at Elizabeth. 'They can fit you in at three o' clock tomorrow.'

'You're a bastard sometimes, Jay,' she muttered fiercely. 'You'd no right to do that.' She was pink in the face as she spun to face him.

'You haven't still got that phobia about going to the doctor, have you?' he asked suddenly.

'No!' Her face was extremely pink now. 'I don't know what you are talking about.'

He smiled. 'At least you've got colour back in your face.'

'I'm not going to that doctor,' she said firmly.

'Why?'

'Because…because I'll go when I'm ready, not when you tell me.'

A glint of amusement was in Jay's eyes for a moment. 'You're a damn stubborn woman, Elizabeth Hammond,' he said wryly.

'And you're overbearing.'

'Someone's got to take control,' he said, his lips twitching. 'Otherwise you'll be eight months' gone and you'll be telling me it's nothing…just something you ate.'

'Don't be ridiculous.'

He picked up the box from the bed and handed it to her. 'Go into the bathroom and do the test.'

'I will when you leave.'

'You must be joking.' He walked across towards the minibar and flicked through the contents. 'I'll have a drink out on the patio while I'm waiting.' He picked up a bottle of beer and the room key that she had thrown down. 'Give me a call when you're ready.'

Then calmly and quietly he closed the door behind him.

CHAPTER ELEVEN

SHE continued to stare at the door for a while after he had left the room. Just who in the hell did he think he was? Of all the high-handed, arrogant men she had ever met, he was the worst.

Well she wasn't going to test herself to order for him, that was for sure. She took the box and headed into the bathroom, bolting the door behind her. She'd stay in here all night if necessary, sleep in the bath. With a bit of luck Cheryl would come and rescue her. She'd send Jay away with a flea in his ear...wouldn't she?

She remembered the look of absolute determination on Jay's face as he'd handed her the box. On the other hand she might have to stay in here for a very long time indeed.

This was absurd. She should go out there herself and order him to go away. Call one of the security guards or something.

She went and looked at her reflection in the mirror. She looked dreadful. Was she pregnant? She stared down at the box in her hand. She was terrified to do the test. What would she feel like if the answer were positive? What would she do?

Maybe she should do the test now, while Jay was waiting...didn't he deserve to know the truth? She felt so mixed up...so scared.

Then she remembered the gentleness of his arms as he'd held her and told her she didn't have to be on her own.

With trembling hands she opened the box.

Jay finished his beer and put the bottle down on the table. He glanced at his watch, then back out to sea. She seemed to have been in there a long time. The blurb on the box had said the result would be instant. He felt nervous...and kind of helpless. Like a child waiting for an exam result, a child promised lots of goodies if the result was good and punishment if it wasn't.

He shouldn't have pushed her into doing the test. He was too damned impatient sometimes.

The door opened behind him and he spun around. She stood in the doorway, a look of uncertainty on her face.

'Well?' He stepped forward.

'Well...I did the test.' She walked past him to lean against the rail.

The sea was only a few metres away. She watched it gently swish against the white beach. A little breeze stirred the palm trees and whispered over her skin gently, soothingly. She took a deep breath.

He was watching her intently, his eyes taking in everything about her. It was unnerving. 'You're off the hook.' She said the words lightly.

'You're not pregnant?'

'You sound disappointed.' She turned to look at him then, her heart beating wildly against her chest.

'Yes, I am.'

'I conned you into marrying me once. I can't trap you into staying with me.' She said the words that were drumming through her consciousness without being aware she had spoken aloud for a minute.

She saw the look of perplexity on the handsome face. 'That's a crazy thing to say. I'd have given anything for you to be pregnant, just so I could have some excuse to try and keep you here.'

She looked up at him, startled out of her reverie. 'Why?'

'Because I love you,' he said quietly, his eyes holding hers. 'And I'd do anything for you.'

She shook her head, wondering if she was hearing things.

'I've been standing here, praying that the answer was going to be positive.' His voice was deep and velvet to her ears. 'I'm devastated.'

'Devastated that I'm not pregnant?' She raked a hand through her hair. 'Because you want me to stay?'

He nodded. There was no doubting the look of disappointment on his face.

'You've never told me you loved me before...' Her voice was stiff, totally unlike herself. 'All the times you held me, made love to me, you never said those words.' A tear threatened to roll down her cheek.

He shrugged. 'You didn't want to hear them.'

'I did!' Her eyes were wide and as blue as the sky above them. 'I longed to hear them.'

'Elizabeth, you were always strongly assertive about the fact that we had a business deal. "A suitable arrangement". Isn't that how you referred to our marriage? You stressed that point from the moment you first proposed. I had to fight to get you into my bed, never mind declare undying love to you.'

'That's not true!'

'Oh, come on, Elizabeth, you know it is. You hid behind business jargon. Said we had to stay together to make it look like a real marriage...so that we'd be sure to get the boat yard.'

'Only because I knew you didn't really want me! I had my pride, Jay Hammond.' Her voice shook with anger. 'You never took the slightest bit of notice of me; you were too busy running around chasing women. When I suggested marriage you nearly fell off your chair with shock.'

'Well, yes, I did.' He grinned. 'But you have to admit it was a bit of an unusual proposal...wasn't it?'

'You didn't want me, though...did you? Not even with

the gift of the yard on my head.' Her voice trembled bitterly.

'Of course I wanted you.' His voice was gentle, perplexed. 'There would have had to be something wrong with me not to want you....didn't I prove that to you on our wedding night?' His voice dipped to a husky, sensual whisper that set her pulses racing.

'You never asked me out.' She kept her voice cool and steady with difficulty. 'Never made a pass at me before the day I asked you to marry me.'

He smiled. 'Because you had ''serious'' written in capital letters all over you,' he murmured. 'I knew if I touched you...if I kissed you, there would be no going back. And I kept telling myself that I didn't want a serious relationship ever again.' He shrugged, his manner self-deprecating. 'I suppose, if I'm honest, I was scared as hell of making another commitment...scared of failing at another relationship. That's why I just played the field. It seemed safer.' His eyes moved gently over her upturned face and he smiled. 'But I wanted you from the moment I first saw you.'

'Now I know you're lying,' she grated fiercely. 'The first moment you saw me, you were in the process of kissing another woman.'

He smiled at that. 'But I was kissing the wrong woman. I looked up, I saw you and...that was it. Life would never be the same again.'

Elizabeth shook her head. 'I don't know why you are saying this, Jay. But I know it's not true.' Her eyes narrowed on him. 'Do you want to be a father so badly that you'd say anything to keep me here? Is that it?'

He shook his head. 'Anyone would think you were the one who had been divorced once before. That you were the one left for someone else. It took me a long time to get over that, Beth. A long time to be able to trust a woman again. And, yes, I did run around with a lot of girlfriends before we got together. But none of them meant anything.'

'Because you were still in love with your ex-wife?' she ventured.

'That's just nonsense.' He came closer to her. 'When I got that divorce I felt like I'd failed. But, looking back, I think it was my pride that hurt more than anything. I told myself that I'd never take the plunge again, that I wasn't cut out for marriage anyway. So I played the field.' He shrugged. 'And I tried to keep my distance from you.'

'You didn't even notice me,' she maintained firmly.

'Yes, I did.' He smiled. 'First time I ever saw you, you were wearing a white dress. And when you stood in certain lights I could see straight through it. I could see the long length of your legs and the lacy curves of your underwear. And I used to want to touch you so badly that I had to go home and have a cold shower.'

She remembered that dress, remembered discovering it was see-through and never wearing it again. She'd thrown it out years ago. Had she been wearing it the day she first met Jay? She couldn't remember and she was sure Jay couldn't either. 'When we talked about this in London, you couldn't remember the woman you were kissing...do you honestly expect me to believe you can recall what I was wearing?'

'Believe what you want,' he said casually. 'But the fact is, I used to watch you and I used to want you. We'd have a beer together after work sometimes and I'd ask if you were seeing someone. I was always relieved when you said you weren't. When you had a date I wanted to tell you to cancel them. I wanted to tell the guy to stay away. I was eaten alive with jealously.'

'You weren't in the slightest bit bothered.' She shook her head, her heart hammering. 'If you had been you would have asked me out yourself.'

'Yeah…well there's the rub.' He shook his head, a derisive smile at his lips. 'You were the danger zone. I knew that if I started to date you…if I kissed you…it would be serious. And I'd promised myself I wasn't going for serious again. To make matters worse you were a nice girl, and you were the boss's daughter. And he was a man I happened to admire and respect. I couldn't play with your affections. Couldn't risk hurting you…getting it wrong.' He looked at her, his eyes dark and intently serious. 'I deliberately gave you a wide berth when it came to romance. But you don't know the self-control I had to exert in order not to make a pass at you.'

'When I asked you to marry me, you had to think long and hard about it… You're not telling me that you were in love with me then, because I remember the look in your eye when I said it. You were horrified.'

He reached and touched the side of her face with a gentle hand. 'You caught me off guard. That was all.'

'I should never have asked you,' she murmured.

'I was glad you did,' he whispered, his eyes lingering on her lips. 'In a way it was like one of those cards you pick up in Monopoly. "Get out of jail free". I got to marry you without having to make the decision. Without having to break the promises I'd made to myself about getting heavily involved again.'

'You mean, I was your safety net?' Her voice trembled alarmingly. 'You could have affairs to your heart's content and break them off using me as your excuse?'

'No!' He looked appalled.

'Oh, come on, Jay, isn't that what you were playing at with Lisa?'

'My affair with Lisa was before we got married,' he said quickly.

'I saw you together.' Elizabeth tried very hard to keep

those words steady, not to fling them at him in fury, but it took all her restraint.

'When?' He frowned.

'Before I left. You were at the office working late with her. Well, you were supposed to be working…' She trailed off derisively. 'You have a penchant for having your girl-friends on your office desk, don't you, Jay?'

She made to turn away from him, but he caught hold of her and swung her back.

'Hold on a moment. You can't fling that one at me and turn away. I didn't have Lisa on my office desk, as you so quaintly put it. She kissed me and I told her very firmly that I was in love with my wife.'

'Did that make it more exciting?'

She watched the colour rise under his skin and wondered suddenly if she had gone too far. He looked furious.

'I did not have an affair with Lisa Cunningham when we were together,' he reiterated strongly. 'I did, however, take her out a few times after you left. I thought that was what you were talking about when you flung her name at me on the beach the other night.'

She stared at him, her heart thumping uncomfortably against her chest. 'Oh, come on, Beth. I'm telling you the truth. I swear.'

'But I heard her talking about your affair. It was one night when we were out at the polo club. I was in the ladies' room and she was telling her friend all about you…how good you were in bed. How you didn't love me. That it was an arranged marriage and you were un-happy and it was only a matter of time before you left me—'

'So you decided to get out first?' Jay guessed.

She nodded. 'It made me realise what a mistake I'd made—'

'And you left me because of that?' Jay asked furiously. 'Well, she was lying, God damn it!'

'How did she know we had an arranged marriage for business reasons?'

'I don't know, but it wasn't anything I'd told her.' Jay's voice was so cold, so contemptuous, that she hesitated.

'Can't you just listen to me? I love you, Elizabeth. And when I married you I wanted it to be for life. I'd do anything to keep you here, with or without the question of the baby.'

When he'd married her, had he intended it to be for life? She'd never believed that. She'd always assumed that he saw their union as short term.

'Why did you ask me to leave?' she asked suddenly.

'Because I overheard you telling Cheryl that you didn't love me and without love our relationship wouldn't work. It angered me, Beth...it floored me as well. I suddenly thought, What the hell is the point of trying?'

'I like you when you're trying.' She gave an uneven smile, her eyes glistening with tears.

'And I can be very trying?' For a moment humour was a shadow in his dark eyes.

'Something like that.' She wanted to kiss him, suddenly. Kiss him and hold him tight.

'And for your information I've never had a mistress. I happen to believe in the sanctity of marriage. Yes, I took Lisa out for lunch a couple of times while you were in London.' He shrugged. 'I was missing you and she was sympathetic. It was a mistake. I realised that when she tried to be too sympathetic. But I didn't follow through...I didn't make love to her. If you must know, I haven't touched another woman since our wedding day...and nor do I want to.'

She stared at him, her heart thumping. It was hard not

to believe him: he said those words with such honesty, such emotion.

'Say it again,' she whispered softly.

'Which part?' He reached out a hand and wiped a tear from her face.

'The "I love you" part.' She smiled tremulously.

'I love you.' He came closer and kissed away the wetness of her tears. 'More than I've ever loved anyone before.'

'I love you too.' She whispered unevenly.

'Do you?'

'Yes…madly, crazily completely. Just like I did on the day I asked you to marry me.'

'You weren't thinking straight back then,'

'I was thinking how much I wanted you.'

'Not how much you wanted the yard?'

She shook her head. 'The yard was only ever an excuse. I knew I could have it anyway. Cheryl had told me that.'

Jay frowned. 'You mean…it wasn't the reason you wanted to get married?'

'I'm sorry—'

She didn't have a chance to say more because suddenly he was kissing her again and for a while they were so wrapped up in each other that she couldn't think of anything else.

When they pulled apart they were both trembling with desire, clinging to each other.

'Elizabeth, don't go back to London. Please.' He looked earnestly into her eyes. 'My life is nothing without you.'

'You can have the yard—' she ventured cautiously.

'Oh, to hell with the damned yard. Part of the reason I wanted you to sell out to me was that it always seemed to be like a wedge between us. Part of me was even a bit jealous of it.'

'What, of an old boat yard?' She stared at him in astonishment.

'It seemed to mean more to you than anything else after your father died.'

'It never meant more to me than you...' she said quickly. 'Do what you want with it...it's you I care about.'

'I'd rather do what I want with you,' he growled against her ear, teasingly, playfully.

'That sounds interesting.' She grinned.

'What about your job in London?'

'I can get another job...I can't get another you so easily.'

'Flattery will get you everywhere,' he said, kissing her firmly, passionately.

'So what do you want to do with me?' she asked teasingly as he pulled back. 'It sounded exciting.'

He thought for a moment, his manner suddenly serious.

'I want you to stay here with me and be my wife,' he said seriously, looking deep into her eyes.

For a moment she was transported back to their wedding day. When they had stood on this beach at eleven and vowed to love and honour until the end of time.

'No secrets, only honesty and love between us from now on.'

'Ah! There is just one thing,' she said softly. 'I haven't been entirely honest with you.'

'Oh...?' He stared at her warily.

'It's about the results of that test.'

'Yes...?'

'If it's a boy, do you think we could call him Alex?'

The world's bestselling romance series.

HARLEQUIN®
Presents

Seduction and Passion Guaranteed!

She's his in the bedroom,
but he can't buy her love...

**MISTRESS
TO A
MILLIONAIRE**

**The ultimate fantasy becomes
a reality in Harlequin Presents®**

Live the dream with more
Mistress to a Millionaire titles
by your favorite authors.

Coming in May

THE ITALIAN'S TROPHY MISTRESS
by Diana Hamilton #2321

**Pick up a Harlequin Presents® novel and you will
enter a world of spine-tingling passion and
provocative, tantalizing romance!**

Available wherever Harlequin Books are sold.

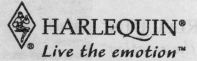

HARLEQUIN®
Live the emotion™

Visit us at www.eHarlequin.com

HPMTAMIL

USA TODAY *bestselling author*

JULIE KENNER

Brings you a supersexy tale of love and mystery...

SILENT CONFESSIONS

A BRAND-NEW NOVEL.

Detective Jack Parker needs an education from a historical sex expert in order to crack his latest case—and bookstore owner Veronica Archer is just the person to help him. But their private lessons give Ronnie some other ideas on how the detective can help *her* sexual education....

"JULIE KENNER JUST MIGHT WELL BE THE MOST ENCHANTING AUTHOR IN TODAY'S MARKET."
—THE ROMANCE READER'S CONNECTION

Look for
SILENT CONFESSIONS,
available in April 2003.

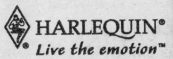

HARLEQUIN®
Live the emotion™

Visit us at www.eHarlequin.com

PHSC

The world's bestselling romance series.

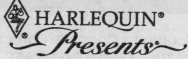

HARLEQUIN®
Presents

Seduction and Passion Guaranteed!

Coming soon from the internationally bestselling author
Penny Jordan

Arabian Nights

An enthralling new duet set in the desert kingdom of Zuran.

THE SHEIKH'S VIRGIN BRIDE
Petra is in Zuran to meet her grandfather—
only to discover he's arranged for her to
marry the rich, eligible Sheikh Rashid!
Petra plans to ruin her own reputation
so that he won't marry her—and asks
Blaize, a gorgeous man at her hotel, to
pose as her lover. Then she makes a
chilling discovery: Blaize is none other
than Sheikh Rashid himself!
On sale June, #2325

ONE NIGHT WITH THE SHEIKH
The attraction between Sheikh
Xavier Al Agir and Mariella Sutton is instant
and all-consuming. But as far as Mariella
is concerned, this man is off-limits. Then
a storm leaves her stranded at the sheikh's
desert home and passion takes over. It's a
night she will never forget....
On sale July, #2332

**Pick up a Harlequin Presents® novel and you will enter a world
of spine-tingling passion and provocative, tantalizing romance!**

Available wherever Harlequin books are sold.

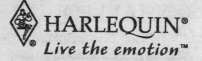

HARLEQUIN®
Live the emotion™

Visit us at www.eHarlequin.com

HPAN2

Welcome to Cooper's Corner....
Some come for pleasure,
others for passion—
and one to set things straight....

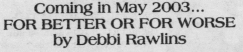

Coming in May 2003...
FOR BETTER OR FOR WORSE
by Debbi Rawlins

Check-in: Veterinarian Alex McAllister is the man to go to in Cooper's Corner for sound advice. But since his wife's death eight years ago, his closest relationship has been with his dog... until he insists on "helping" Jenny Taylor by marrying her!

Checkout: Jenny has a rare illness, and as Alex's wife her medical costs would be covered. But Jenny doesn't want a marriage based on gratitude...she wants Alex's love!

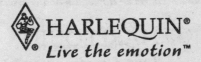

HARLEQUIN®
Live the emotion™

Visit us at www.eHarlequin.com

CC-CNM10

A "Mother of the Year" contest brings
overwhelming response as thousands of women
vie for the luxurious grand prize....

Kate Hoffmann

Jacqueline Diamond

Jill Shalvis

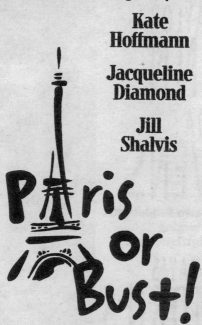

Paris or Bust!

A hilarious and romantic trio of new stories!

With a trip to Paris at stake, these women are
determined to win! But the laughs are many as three of
them discover that being finalists isn't the most
excitement they'll ever have.... Falling in love is!

Available in April 2003.

HARLEQUIN®
Makes any time special®

Visit us at www.eHarlequin.com

PHPOB

Forgetting the past can destroy the future...

TARA TAYLOR QUINN

AMANDA STEVENS

Bring you two full-length novels of riveting romantic intrigue in...

YESTERDAY'S MEMORIES

Two people struggle to regain their memories while rediscovering past loves, in this gripping volume of reading.

Look for it in May 2003— wherever books are sold.

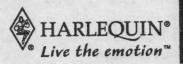

HARLEQUIN®
Live the emotion™

Visit us at www.eHarlequin.com

BR2YM

Three romantic comedies that will have you laughing out loud!

Favorite Harlequin Temptation® author

Stephanie Bond

brings you...

✳*LOVESTRUCK*✳

Three full-length novels of romance...
and the humorous missteps that often accompany it!

Get LOVESTRUCK in June 2003—wherever books are sold.

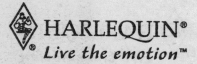

HARLEQUIN®
Live the emotion™

Visit us at www.eHarlequin.com

BR3L

The world's bestselling romance series.

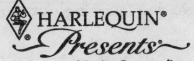

HARLEQUIN®
Presents®

Seduction and Passion Guaranteed!

*Getting down to business
in the boardroom...
and the bedroom!*

*A secret romance,
a forbidden affair,
a thrilling attraction...*

What happens when two people work together
and simply can't help falling in love—no matter
how hard they try to resist?

Find out in

BACK IN THE BOSS'S BED
by Sharon Kendrick
On sale May, #2322

Pick up a
Harlequin Presents®
novel and you will
enter a world of
spine-tingling passion
and provocative,
tantalizing romance!

Available wherever Harlequin Books are sold.

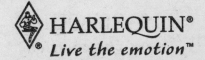

HARLEQUIN®
Live the emotion™

Visit us at www.eHarlequin.com

HPNTFAP